THE CORPSE MOVED UPSTAIRS

When Johnny Fletcher found a corpse in his trunk, he was sure he could solve the case. Then one murder turned into two, the beautiful blonde lied to him, and the real secret turned out to be somewhere in Iowa.

Books by Frank Gruber
in the Linford Mystery Library:

THE HONEST DEALER
THE ETRUSCAN BULL
THE TALKING CLOCK
MURDER ONE
THE FRENCH KEY
BROTHERS OF SILENCE
MARKET FOR MURDER

FRANK GRUBER

THE CORPSE MOVED UPSTAIRS

Complete and Unabridged

LINFORD
Leicester

First published in the
United States of America as
'THE MIGHTY BLOCKHEAD'

First Linford Edition
published August 1992

British Library CIP Data

Gruber, Frank
The corpse moved upstairs.—Large print ed.—
Linford mystery library
I. Title II. Series
823.912 [F]

ISBN 0–7089–7236-5

Published by
F. A. Thorpe (Publishing) Ltd.
Anstey, Leicestershire

Set by Words & Graphics Ltd.
Anstey, Leicestershire
Printed and bound in Great Britain by
T. J. Press (Padstow) Ltd., Padstow, Cornwall

1

JOHNNY FLETCHER had the key in his hand, but it wasn't necessary to put it in the lock, for the door was slightly ajar. He pushed it open and said over his shoulder:

"This mousetrap gets scrummier right along. The maids don't even bother to lock the rooms any more after cleaning up."

Sam Cragg grunted as he followed Johnny Fletcher into the room. "If you worked oftener we wouldn't have to stay at dumps like this." He took off his coat and, throwing it on one of the twin beds, plumped himself down into an armchair. It creaked under his 200 pounds. "At that, we're in better condition than we usually are when we get to New York. We've got eight dollars between us and a bunch of books — "

1

"And a trunk!" Johnny nodded toward the black, rivet-studded trunk that stood in one corner of the room. He grinned. "That was one of my more brilliant ideas, Sam. You go into a hotel with a couple of paper cartons containing books and they don't consider that baggage, so they ask for the room rent in advance. But you put the same books into a trunk and they give you a nice, pleasant smile. A man who owns a trunk is a substantial citizen. And it only cost us six dollars, secondhand."

"Trunk or no trunk," said Sam Cragg, "if Peabody'd been on the job today, I don't think he'd let us have this room without laying it on the line."

Johnny Fletcher chuckled. "Maybe we'd better get a handful of money. It'll disappoint him no end if we're able to pay. Break out some books and we'll take a look-see around Times Square."

Sam Cragg got up and went to the

trunk. He lifted the lid and uttered a cry of horror.

"Johnny, for cripes sakes!"

He let the trunk lid bang down.

Johnny Fletcher took a quick step toward Sam Cragg, then stopped as he caught the full significance of his friend's distorted, shocked face.

"What — what's in the trunk?"

"A dead man!"

"What?"

Johnny reached past Sam, gripped the trunk lid and jerked it up. He looked down into the trunk, holding onto the lid and it seemed to him that all the strength flowed from his lean body to the floor. Sam Cragg jostled him and Johnny felt the shudder that shook Sam.

"Gee?"

Gently, Johnny let down the lid. Then he turned to Sam, his nostrils flaring.

"What became of the books?"

"Eh? What?"

"The books aren't in the trunk;

where are they?" Johnny tried to answer the question himself by dropping to the floor and shooting a swift look under the beds and cheap chiffonier. Then he got up and strode to the clothes closet.

He looked inside and whistled softly. Then he whirled and gave Sam a startled look.

"The clothes in the closet, they don't belong to us. And the trunk," he darted a scrutinizing glance at it; "it isn't ours!"

Sam Cragg lumbered forward. "Holy cow! It ain't!"

"Of course not. It's the same size and style as ours, but it's newer. I should have noticed that before, but . . . " Johnny inhaled suddenly and rushed to the door. He jerked it open, swung it shut and came back to Sam.

Consternation was spread over his face. "We're in the wrong room, Sam!"

"What! How could we?"

"This is *seven* twenty-one. Our room is eight twenty-one. Cripes, the rooms are the same. The elevator operator made a mistake and let us off on the seventh floor and we didn't notice. The door was open and I didn't have to use the key. And neither of us thought to look at the number on the — "

"What're we waiting for?" cried Sam Cragg. "Come on!"

But Johnny Fletcher beat him to the door and held him back a moment while he listened. Not hearing any sound in the corridor, he opened the door cautiously. He stuck out his head, then stepped out.

Sam closed the door quietly and followed Johnny. The staircase was beside the elevator, some twenty feet from Room 721. Johnny had reached it and was taking the first step up the carpeted flight, when he heard a door slam somewhere on the seventh floor. He jerked about to hurry Sam, but it was an unnecessary movement. Sam hurled past him, taking three stairs in one jump.

Ten seconds later they both reached

the eight floor level and Johnny unlocked Room 821 with the room key. His eyes went instantly to the black trunk in the corner and he felt better when he saw it. But he was not satisfied completely until he had raised the lid and found the trunk filled with books.

Sam, looking over Johnny's shoulder shuddered in relief. "Gee, what a narrow escape!"

"Escape, Sam?"

"Yeah, sure. Imagine if the stiff'd been in *our* trunk and *our* room. What would we have done with it?"

"I don't know. That was the first time I ever found a dead man in a trunk, a murdered man."

"Murdered? What . . . how do you know he was murdered?" Sam looked a little sick.

"The left side of his head was all bashed in."

Sam groaned. "Don't, Johnny! It's bad enough just thinking about it. Gee, what I'd give for a drink!"

Johnny brightened. "*That's* what *I* need! Come on, what're we waiting for?"

Johnny locked the door behind them, then pressed the button for the elevator. It came after a moment and as the door opened, Johnny nudged Sam cautiously.

As the elevator dropped to the lobby floor, Johnny whistled a few bars of 'Silver Threads Among the Gold.' He winked at the elevator operator as he stepped out to the lobby. "Great song!"

Without looking toward the desk, Johnny and Sam left the hotel. On the sidewalk, they turned left toward Seventh Avenue. A half block up the street was Dinky Maquire's Pretzel Parlor.

They went in. There was sawdust on the floor and a long bar stretching down the length of the narrow room. The bar was being held up by a solid line of afternoon customers. Halfway down the room, a pasty-faced youth with a cigarette glued to his lips was pounding a midget piano. A blowsy blonde was holding up the midget piano and wailing something about: 'This little piggy went to market.'

Johnny saw a small opening at the bar and attacked it. He was having poor luck widening the salient, until Sam Cragg threw his burly, muscular body into the breach and with a shove or two made room for both himself and Johnny.

"Two beers," Johnny said to the bartender.

"Beer?" Sam scowled. "I thought we were going to have a drink."

"You know what happened the last time you had anything stronger than beer? Excuse me."

The last to a man on his left who was about four drinks beyond his quota. He waved an old fashioned so that it sloshed over his hand. "I said to quit shovin'. I don't like to be shoved aroun', see?"

Sam Cragg grinned pleasantly past Johnny. "Nobody's shoving you around, buddy."

"The hell they ain't. I'm sick and tired of bein' shoved aroun' and the next guy that tries it is goin' to get a smack in the kisser, see?"

A man on the far side of the inebriated one tugged at his elbow. "Cut it out, Ken, nobody's shoving you."

Ken brushed off the hand and his elbow and took a swing at Johnny Fletcher, which missed by a foot and grazed Sam Cragg's shoulder. Sam grabbed Ken's wrist and brought it down.

The drunk swung with his other hand. Sam rolled his head and caught the second wrist. He put it with the first and held both with one hand.

"Naughty, naughty, " he chided.

"Leggo," howled Ken. "Leggo, or I'll knock your head off."

"Knock ahead," Sam invited cheerfully. He leaned carelessly against the bar; while he held the struggling drunk's wrists with his one hand.

By this time the scuffle had attracted the attention of almost everyone along the bar and they were crowding around so thick the official tavern bouncer had a hard time breaking through the ring. But he finally succeeded.

"Hey," he exclaimed. "Cut it out."

The drunk's friend was hopping up and down, trying to get at Sam Cragg to rescue Ken, but Johnny Fletcher blocked him successfully. Now Johnny sidestepped to face the bouncer, who was holding his right hand behind his back. This to Johnny's experienced eye indicated either a blackjack or brass knuckles. "We didn't start this," Johnny said, "but if you butt in someone's going to get hurt."

"Sure," said the bouncer. "You!" He brought out his hand. There was a set of brass knuckles on the fist.

Sam Cragg pushed Ken, the drunk, so violently against the bouncer that the latter went down backwards, the drunk on top of him. Sam stooped and catching the bouncer's hand striped the brass from it. Then he jerked the bouncer to his feet and slapped him with his open palm. The man's head rocked and his knees buckled. Sam let him fall.

"Gee!" said the friend of the drunk. "Blockhead, the Strong Man."

"What's you call me?" Sam snapped.

"Blockhead — "

"Blockhead! You want some of what I gave this guy?"

The man backed away. "No, no. I didn't mean that as a insult. I — you know, Blockhead, the famous comic character? I — I work on the magazine."

"Oh," said Sam.

Johnny nudged Sam. "I think it's time to beat it. The barkeep's telephoned for John Law. Gangway, folks, the fun's over."

A lane was quickly made for them and Johnny and Sam reached the door. They were none too soon, for they had

11

scarcely cleared it when a uniformed policeman came tearing around the corner nearby and bore down on Dinky Maquire's Pretzel Parlor.

Johnny and Sam walked swiftly to the door of the 45th Street Hotel. They stepped into the elevator and made sure this time that they got off at the eight floor.

Inside their room Johnny said petulantly, "That was a fine glass of beer we didn't have."

"I said we ought to move away from this street," Sam groused. "It's got so you can't do anything any more. This hotel . . . "

Johnny nodded, his face creased in annoyance. "I'm ready to move; all we need's the dough."

"That's what *I* said. One good pitch and we'd have it."

"Now you're talking, Johnny." Sam went eagerly to the big trunk. As he put his hands on the lid Johnny said drily, "Be funny if there'd be a corpse in this one."

12

"Funny," said Sam. I don't — " He lifted the lid. His hoarse cry caused Johnny to whirl and leap to his side. One glance into the trunk and Johnny leaped to the door. He jerked it open, stared at the number on the door and came back.

"It's *our* room!"

2

SAM had already let the lid fall back on the trunk. He reeled away. "It can't be, Johnny."

"It is. And it's our trunk this time. But what . . . " He strode to the door of the clothes closet and pulled it open. Stack upon stack of books were piled on the floor.

He stared at them and Sam came and breathed hoarsely down his collar. "Gee, they took the books out of the trunk an' — "

"We're drunk, Sam," said Johnny slowly.

"But we didn't drink anything!"

"Then we're crazy. This *couldn't* happen. This is the same stiff that was in Room 721 a half hour ago. How could it have got up here in *our* room?"

Sam clapped a hand to his broad

14

forehead. "We're sunk, Johnny. The cops!"

"The cops, yeah, the cops." A shudder ran through Johnny Fletcher. "All right, let's get it out of here."

"What?"

"The stiff. We can't keep it in our trunk, can we? For all we know the cops may already be on their way here. We've got to get rid of it!"

"How? Where can we ditch it?"

"I don't know, but . . . " Johnny Fletcher's eyes darted around to the window, which opened on a courtyard. Sam Cragg, watching Johnny, winced.

"No, Johnny."

"No, I guess not. Just the same, you'd better pull down the window shade."

Sam obeyed. When he turned from the window he saw Johnny opening the trunk lid once more. Sam remained by the window until Johnny called to him.

"The hell with them, Sam. They can't park their corpses in *our* room.

15

We'll take it back."

"Back to — to Room 721?"

"That's right."

Sam cried out. "Johnny, the chances!"

"Stay here. I'll go investigate. Don't leave the room."

Sam shuddered and crowded forward. "I'll go with you."

"No," Johnny said, sharply. "Stand by the door, with your shoulder against it. Just in case." Before Sam could protest further Johnny pulled open the door and stepped out.

There was no one in the corridor. He walked casually to the elevator, looked around, then darted to the staircase. He took the carpeted stairs two at a time.

The corridor of the seventh floor was also empty. Johnny's eyes narrowed and he stepped to the door of Room 721. With his hand reaching for it he stopped. The door was slightly ajar. He was sure he and Sam had closed it after their precipitate departure.

But of course. Someone had been inside since then — and out again.

He took another step toward the door. Inside the room, someone hummed softly. Johnny strained his ears. The humming was definitely feminine.

Johnny raised his hand and rapped lightly on the door. The humming stopped and a woman's voice called, "Yes?"

Johnny mumbled something unintelligible. The woman inside came to the door, pulled it open.

Johnny did not have to pretend surprise. The girl who faced him was beautiful enough to be a Powers model. She was tall and slender, with a fair complexion and the most gorgeously golden-blond hair Johnny had ever seen.

He blinked. "Uh, isn't this Mr. Cragg's room?"

The girl smiled and shook her head. "Definitely not, and your technique is old fashioned. Scram!"

"Believe it or not," Johnny grinned. "My pal, Cragg, had this room this morning, eight twenty-one."

"This is *seven* twenty-one and do you go quietly or do I call the house dick?"

"Okay," Johnny conceded, "but you can't blame a guy, can you?"

The blonde made a brushing motion with her hand. "I work for a living and I know too many Johns now."

"Bingo! *My* name is John. Johnny to my pals. Johnny Fletcher. And you?"

"Jill. Whoa! I said *ixnay*." The girl closed the door firmly in Johnny's face. He heard the bolt shoot on the inside. He nodded quietly, then turned and headed back to the stairs.

He stepped up close to the door of Room 821. "All right, Sam."

Sam opened the door a crack, peered out, then opened the door. Johnny did not step in. "Bring it," he said.

Sam's face recoiled as if Johnny had struck it. "Huh?"

"Hurry, we haven't all day."

Sam disappeared. But a moment later Johnny heard his deep breathing and pushed in the door. He stepped

18

back quietly and darted another look up and down the corridor. Then he nodded.

Sam followed Johnny, carrying the gruesome object. Johnny went to the stairs, but, instead of going down, went up this time. Sam followed. At the top of the flight, Johnny held Sam back, while he reconnoitered. Then he stepped quickly across the corridor and jerked open the door of the linen closet, next to the door of Room 921.

He gestured to Sam and the latter crossed the open space and stooping set down the body. Johnny let the door swing shut.

"Okay."

They hurried back to their own room Sam locked the door on the inside and went to the bathroom to wash his hands and mop the perspiration from his face. When he came out he found Johnny piling books into the trunk.

"I've aged fifteen years, Johnny," Sam said wearily. "And I don't think

I'll ever be able to open another trunk as long as I live."

"That was about the dirtiest trick we ever had played on us," Johnny declared," and when I get the guy who did it — "

"No!" Sam cried. "You ain't — you ain't figurin' on playing detective again, are you?"

"I don't like dead men being stuffed into my trunk."

Sam groaned and threw himself full length upon the nearest bed. "Here we go again. I knew this joint was a jinx. We shoulda . . . "

A woman's scream tore through the hotel. Sam leaped up from the bed. "Holy cats! What?"

Johnny waved him back. "Lie down, Sam, that's only the chambermaid finding the stuff. It's a dirty trick on her, but if she'd been on the job, *we* wouldn't have found it — twice! Now, let's see how long it takes the cops to get here."

He put the last of the books into the

trunk and slammed down the lid. Then he went to the far bed and stretched out on it. He stared at the dingy ceiling.

Doors were opening and closing in the corridors. Feet hurried across the worn rugs and the elevators were humming continuously.

On the bed next to Johnny's, Sam Cragg trembled. "I still think we shouldda scrammed outta here, Johnny. You know how Peabody is; anything used to happen around here he blamed us for it."

"Ah, Peabody," said Johnny.

Knuckles rapped light on the door, Johnny called, "Who is it?"

"Me, Eddie Miller."

"Come!"

A slender, sharp-faced youth in the smart uniform of bellboy opened the door. "Hi, Mr. Fletcher; Sammy Cragg! I heard you checked in."

"Greetings, Eddie," said Johnny. "How've you been?"

21

"So-so, Mr. Fletcher. Things been quiet around the joint. I knew they'd pick up with you back."

Johnny raised his head and looked over the big mound that was Sam Cragg on the adjoining twin bed. "That has all the earmarks of a crack, Eddie."

The bellboy grinned. "Uh-uh, Mr. Fletcher. I'm on *your* side. Only ten minutes ago, Mr. Peabody got back from a hotel managers' convention and saw your names on the register. You shouldda heard him howl."

"I did. His voice sounded like a woman's who's just seen a mouse."

"That was a woman. Mmm, Gussie, the chambermaid, right above you on the ninth floor. She found a dead man in the linen closet."

Johnny Fletcher exclaimed. "What a dump! First thing you know they'll be planting corpses in the guests' rooms."

"Mmm," said Eddie Miller. "Could happen. Well, I just thought I'd tip you off about Peabody."

"Why, Eddie?"

"Oh, I dunno. I just thought well, you know, and you and him never got along so well."

"We'll see you around, Eddie. By the way, what's the name of the good-looking blonde right under us. I saw her in the elevator."

"Yeah? Don't blame you, Mr. Fletcher. She's a pip. Her name's Jill Thayer. She's an artist."

"An artist? She doesn't look it."

"Well, I guess you'd really call her a cartoonist. She draws funny pictures. But you've got competition there. She's got a boy friend lives here at the hotel. Name of Ken Ballinger. He draws Blockhead."

"Blockhead!" exclaimed Sam Cragg. "What the . . . ?"

Eddie Miller brightened. "D'you read it? I guess everybody does. Swell stuff."

"What," asked Johnny Fletcher, "is Blockhead? Or is it who?"

"Who. Gosh, ain't you seen Block-head, the Strong Man? It's a comic

23

strip, runs in all the newspapers and you see him on TV and in the movies. Then there's the magazine; that's what Ballinger does."

"Can you get me a copy?"

"Sure, it only cost twelve cents. I'll pick it up at the newsstand downstairs. On the cuff?"

"Eh?"

Eddie Miller grinned. "I just wanted to know. Okay, I'll run up with it."

The bellboy slipped out of the room. Sam Cragg started to talk, but Johnny Fletcher placed a finger to his lips and swinging off the bed, said, "Great kid, that Eddie Miller. Probably own this hotel some day."

Noiselessly he stepped to the door and jerked it open. Eddie Miller almost tumbled into the room, but he picked himself up and dusted his knees nonchalantly.

"I was tyin' my shoelace," he said. "Thanks for the recommend, Mr. Fletcher."

"You're welcome, Eddie. Remind

me to talk to my friend, the manager of the Barbizon-Waldorf about you."

"What, again?"

Johnny closed the door and came back into the room. "As I was saying, Eddie Miller'll probably own this hotel some day if he doesn't get killed by one of the guests."

Out in the corridor the elevator door clanged. Voices approached and after a moment, heavy knuckles massaged the door of Room 821.

"Well," Johnny said, "this is it, I guess. Come in, Mr. Peabody!"

The door was shoved inwards and a big square-built man almost filled the doorway. The slender Mr. Peabody, manager of the 45th Street Hotel, peered around from behind the big man.

"Well, well, fellows!" boomed the big man. "Welcome back to the big town. If you'd let me know you were coming I'd have had a paddy wagon meet you at the station."

"Phooey," sniffed Sam Cragg.

But Johnny Fletcher gave the big man the glad hand. "Lieutenant Madigan! How're you, old sock! Bet you've been having a tough time solving your cases without me around. You wouldn't have a nice juicy one on tap that you've been having trouble with?"

"As a matter of fact, Johnny Fletcher," said Lieutenant Madigan of Homicide, "I've got one, right on your doorsteps."

"Mr. Fletcher," Peabody, the hotel manager, cut in, "I just learned that you had checked into the hotel this afternoon. You know the rules — "

"You've told them to me often enough. But I still don't like them. And, Mr. Peabody, I simply must protest about a few things around here. Your elevators are much, much, too noisy. And the maid left only two towels in the bathroom. We wash twice a day, Mr. Peabody."

Mr. Peabody got very red in the face. "If you don't like the service, why do you always come back to this hotel?"

"Because I like *you*, Mr. Peabody. And so does Sam. Don't you Sammy?"

"Yeah!"

Lieutenant Madigan chuckled. "It's a pleasure to hear you ladle it out, Johnny. But to get back to business; when did you and Cragg check in here?"

"This afternoon; why?"

"What time?"

"About one o'clock."

"And you've been in your room ever since?"

Johnny grimaced. "What is this, Maddy? Do we have to register with the police these days?"

"It might be a good idea — in your case. I have a reason for asking."

"You mean because of the stiff upstairs?"

Mr. Peabody yipped, but Lieutenant Madigan said quickly. "How do you know about that, Fletcher?"

"Didn't I hear the yell? I'm not deaf, you know. Anyway, one of the bellboys mentioned it."

"Eddie Miller!" howled Peabody. "I'll fire that boy."

"I'd like to see you try it."

Lieutenant Madigan scowled. "All right, Fletcher. You know about the dead man. What else can you tell me?"

"A chambermaid found the body in the linen closet on the ninth floor. References: the bellboy. That's all."

"Is it? *You* didn't see the body?"

"Should I have?"

"No, but I was wondering how he happened to have one of your books in his hand."

"What?"

"Don't you and Cragg sell a book called *Every Man a Samson*?"

"Of course. That's how we make all the money we pay these hotels."

Mr. Peabody again opened his mouth, but Lieutenant Madigan waved him down. "All right, how'd the dead man get hold of this book?"

"I wouldn't know. We haven't sold any in New York. We only just got back in town. Let's see the book."

"I haven't got it."

"Wouldn't he give it up?"

"As a matter of fact," said Lieutenant Madigan, "he didn't exactly have a book in his hand. But some blood got on his hand and the hand must have got onto the book, because it took off part of the cover, an impression. Where're your books?"

"Why?"

"I'd like to check them over."

"Why?"

"To see if there's any blood on them."

"Are you crazy, Madigan? The body was found upstairs. How would blood from it get on one of my books?"

"That's what I want to find out."

Johnny blinked and shook his head. "My books are in the trunk — naturally. The trunk's been locked ever since the porter brought it up this afternoon."

"Let me have the key."

"Tsk. Tsk. Can you beat it. I lost the key only yesterday."

Lieutenant Madigan bared his teeth. "Then I'll break it open."

"You'll break it open, Lieutenant?" Johnny laughed shortly. "My hundred and fifty-dollar trunk?"

"A hundred and fifty . . . ahrr! Cut it out, Fletcher. You know that's a secondhand cardboard box."

"I say it's worth a hundred and fifty dollars, Lieutenant, and that's what it's going to cost somebody if they break it."

"I'll get a locksmith, Fletcher."

Johnny beamed. "That's better! I don't mind your looking — just as long as you don't break the trunk."

Lieutenant Madigan glowered and turned to the door. "I'll be back in ten minutes; don't try leaving here."

"We won't Madigan, old boy. We're just as curious as you are, aren't we, Sammy?"

"Yeah, sure," grunted Sam Cragg.

Madigan strode out, but Peabody lingered. "Now, Mr. Fletcher, about the rent."

Johnny Fletcher stepped over suddenly and placed the flat of his hand on Mr. Peabody's thin chest. "You heard what the lieutenant said, Peabody? Well?" He shoved suddenly on Mr. Peabody and to prevent himself from falling the hotel manager took two or three quick backward steps, which carried him out into the hall. Johnny closed the door in his face and bolted it.

"Mr. Fletcher!" Peabody cried through the thin door panels.

Johnny whirled into the room. "Quick, Sam, the trunk."

"What? You can't get rid of it."

"The books! Take them out and look them over!"

They both rushed to the trunk and Johnny quickly unlocked it and began handing out books to Sam Cragg. There were more than a hundred in the trunk and they had to work fast. They were more than halfway down before Johnny touched one that was sticky, He grunted and stood it carefully on end and continued the search. Another was found that had blood on it and then near the bottom still another with a tiny red smear.

Johnny took the books to the bathroom and wrapped them in a towel. When he got back Sam had returned most of the volumes to the trunk. Johnny shot a quick look around the room, then stepped to the door. He put his ear to it and heard deep breathing outside. Which was as he had expected. Lieutenant Madigan had put a guard outside the door.

3

HE went to the window. It had grown dark outside, but he could make out the roof of the adjoining six-story building directly across the courtyard. He leaned out of the window and was about to throw the towel-wrapped bundle across the space, when he saw the light of the window directly below — the room of Jill Thayer, the cartoonist.

He frowned. The roof wasn't safe. Madigan was too shrewd not to search it. He slipped off his necktie, got Sam's and tied them together. He tied one end about the bundle, then went again to the window. Leaning out, he lowered the bundle to the top of the window below and let it swing gently so that it knocked the glass.

Almost instantly the girl below came to the window and sticking out her head looked. "Hold this for me, will you?" Johnny called softly.

"Are you crazy?" the girl gasped.

"No," Johnny retorted. "I'm in a jam. The cops, they're outside my door. C'mon be a sport."

Lieutenant Madigan's fist banged the door. "All right, Fletcher, open up!"

Johnny groaned. "They're banging on my door now," he whispered hoarsely. "Grab this — or I'm sunk."

"Come on, Fletcher!" Madigan cried.

Johnny said, "I'm letting go!" And he did.

He turned back to the room, looked at Sam's taut, gray face — and listened. He didn't hear the bundle hit the courtyard floor.

"All right, Sam," he said. "Open the door for the gorilla." Quickly he darted to lock the trunk, then returned and threw himself upon one of the beds.

Sam unlocked the door. "Why don't you break the door down?"

"I would've in a minute." He motioned to a slender, dark-complexioned man who stood in the doorway, "There's the trunk; get it open."

Johnny Fletcher sat up on the bed and yawned. "I must've fallen asleep. Been here long, copper?"

Madigan glowered. "In a couple of minutes I'll talk to you, Fletcher. And maybe you won't enjoy hearing what I'm going to say."

The locksmith took a bunch of keys from his pocket, pawed through them and tried one in the lock of the trunk. The spring lock snapped open. "There you are, officer, a very common type of cheap lock."

"Thanks," snapped Madigan.

He turned to the trunk as a squat thick set man came into the room, "Ah, Foxie!" said Johnny Fletcher.

Detective Fox grimaced. "I'm going to get you guys down at headquarters yet. Maybe this is the time."

"You hope."

"All right, Fox" said Madigan. "You know what to look for." He took out a handful of books. *Every Man a*

Samson," he said sarcastically. "How you sell this crap I don't know."

"How about buying one yourself, Lieutenant?" Johnny asked. "Make you nice and strong — like Sam Cragg."

"No, it wouldn't," Sam cut in. "You got to have something to start with."

"An ox is strong, too," Madigan retorted, "but it hasn't got much brains."

The deeper Madigan got into the books, the more fiercely he scowled. He began scrutinizing the books more closely.

"Don't wear off the covers," Johnny chided, "or we'll have to charge you for them."

Lieutenant Madigan made an unintelligible sound. Johnny Fletcher let him get to the bottom of the trunk, then said, "Just to show you how smart you are, Madigan, is the dead man a midget? 'Cause if he isn't, he couldn't have been in the trunk with all those books."

Madigan straightened. "What?"

Detective Fox looked at his superior with shocked eyes. "He was a big fellow, Lieutenant."

"I saw him," Madigan snapped. His face was reddening and he dropped a handful of books into the trunk. "I still think — "

"You do?" Johnny looked at him mockingly.

With most of the books still piled on the rug outside the trunk, Madigan slammed down the lid. "The hell with you, Fletcher. But remember, I'll be thinking about you. Come on, Fox!"

Johnny waited until they were at the door, then he called, "Thanks for having my trunk opened, Maddy, old boy!"

Lieutenant Madigan slammed the door.

Sam Cragg said, "Whew!" and dropped into the shabby armchair. Johnny grinned in relief. "Kinda fast for a while, but it's okay now, Sam."

"I dunno. I hope so!"

Someone knocked at the door.

"Who is it?" Johnny snapped.

"Bellboy!"

Eddie Miller came in, grinning. He thrust a gaudy magazine at Johnny. "Here she is, Blockhead, the Strong man. Twelve cents and the best twelve cents worth you ever bought. Three million kids can't be wrong."

"Three million — "

"It says right on the cover, 'Three million circulation.' And like I told you, that ain't all. Blockhead runs in 500 newspapers. He's on TV and they got him running in a movie serial over on Eighth Avenue."

Johnny paid the boy. Eddie Miller inspected the coins as if they were some strange specimens.

"Don't you want it?" Johnny snapped.

"Yeah, sure, only . . . so you *are* broke again. Peabody won't like that."

"Yeah. Peabody; he was up here awhile ago. Said something about firing a certain bellboy."

Eddie Miller grinned impudently.

38

"Not me, he won't. I know where the body's buried."

"Where, Eddie?"

"That's telling."

"For how much?"

"You mean it?"

"Sure, it might come in handy. Uh, Peabody has a one-track mind, sometimes."

"You mean about the rent? Well, I dunno if this'll do *you* any good, but he collects french postcards."

Johnny whistled. "Peabody?"

"Uh-huh, and he reads spicy magazines."

"Which ones?" Sam Cragg asked.

Eddie shrugged, "*Racy Stories, Hotsy-Totsy Stories, O Baby* . . . there's a whole raft of them."

"And Peabody reads them. Tsk. Tsk. Interesting, but I don't see how I can make any profit out of it."

"It's worth keeping in mind. Well, I see you made out all right with the cops."

"Why shouldn't we, Eddie?"

"No reason," Eddie said, hastily. "Only I was thinking things don't happen in the hotel when you and Sam are away."

"Thinking is bad — for growing boys, Eddie."

Eddie Miller sniffed. "Growing boy! And me a bellhop for seven years. Mr. Fletcher, I could write a book!"

With an injured air Eddie Miller took his departure. Johnny tossed the copy of *Blockhead* to Sam and reached for the telephone.

"Who you calling, Johnny?" Sam asked.

"Room 721, please," Johnny said into the telephone.

Sam exclaimed, "Nix, Johnny. Let it slide."

"How can I? Hello, Jill? This is Johnny. How about — "

Jill Thayer cut him off "Listen, you lowdown — "

"Eh, eh!" Johnny cried. "Walls have ears, you know. I was wondering if you'd like to inhale a glass of beer down in the cocktail room?"

He could hear her inhale sharply. Then she said, "Can't. I have a date this evening. I was just about to go out."

"This'll only take five minutes. It's — well, you know."

"I don't know, but I'd like to know. Very well, in five minutes, down in the cocktail room!"

"Swell!"

Johnny hung up to meet Sam's accusing eye. "When'd you meet *her*?"

"A while ago. After all, I've got to explain about those books."

"Why?"

"Because. Come on, if you're coming."

Sam rolled up the copy of *Blockhead* and followed Johnny from the room. The latter locked the door carefully.

As they stepped out of the elevator, Mr. Peabody, who was pacing the lobby nervously, bore down on them. "Mr. Fletcher, I want to talk to you."

"I want to talk to *you*, Peabody.

41

What's the idea bringing cops up to our room?"

Peabody gasped. "*I* bring police to *your* room? It's you who brings all this trouble to my hotel."

"Are you nuts? Because the cutthroats who hang out at this dump kill each other, is it my fault?"

"Shh! Not so loud — please! I'm not happy about this at all, Mr. Fletcher."

"I shouldn't think you would be. See you around."

"Wait! There's that other matter — the room rent."

"Baggage, Mr. Peabody," said Johnny. "We've got baggage. You're always hollering about the rules; well, you know that one very well. Guests with luggage don't have to pay in advance."

"But all you've got in your trunk is a bunch of books."

"Show me the rule that says a guest can't carry books in his luggage. Show me that and I'll be very happy to pay a week's rent in advance. Otherwise — see you in a week, huh?"

Johnny winked and headed for the cocktail room.

The place was about what you'd expect in connection with a hotel like the 45th Street, a short bar, a few booths with dim lights and a smell of stale beer.

"Two beers," Johnny said to the bartender as they walked up to the bar.

"Speak for yourself, Johnny," Sam Cragg said peevishly. "After a day like today, I want a scotch and soda."

"Two beers," Johnny repeated.

"Coming up!"

As the bartender put the beer before them, Jill Thayer came into the place. She was wearing a silver lame evening dress, a silver fox cape, and her hair had stardust scattered in it. There was a newspaper-wrapped parcel under her arm.

Johnny whistled softly, "Jill! You're looking more beautiful every day. Allow me to present my friend and assistant, Sam Cragg."

Jill Thayer gave Johnny the cold eye, then shifted it to Sam, after which she moved to one of the booths, some distance from the bar. Johnny carried his glass of beer to the booth and Sam followed.

"Will you have a beer?" Johnny asked.

"Yes," said Jill Thayer. "Waiter! A champagne cocktail."

Johnny winced. "Okay, it's on me. You helped us out of a tight spot."

Jill shoved the parcel across the table. "There, keep it! Now, answer me just one question: what made you think I would accept that — *that* from you?"

"Well," said Johnny, "he was in your room first."

"What?"

"Yep. In your trunk."

"What're you talking about?" Jill exclaimed.

The bartender brought the champagne cocktail at that moment, and Johnny waited until he had gone. Then he said, "I mean, we went into your room a couple of hours ago — by mistake. The elevator operator let us off the wrong floor and we didn't notice until we were inside."

"Wait a minute! How could you get inside my room without a key?"

"The door was unlocked, standing ajar."

"It was locked when I came in at five-thirty."

"Sure. And he wasn't in the trunk then."

"He?" Jill's eyes widened. "What do you mean, he? The . . . "

"The corpse." Johnny said softly. "Your room is exactly like ours and you have a trunk that's almost a twin of our own, except that it's a little newer. We didn't notice that at first. Sam opened your trunk, saw it — and then we scrammed. An hour later we returned to our room and the stiff had been moved from your trunk in your room to our trunk in our room."

Jill just stared at Johnny Fletcher. "Are you crazy?"

"Some people have said so," Johnny admitted. "But just for the fun of it, take a good look in your trunk. If there are no bloodstains . . . "

Jill shuddered. "Admit for the moment that a corpse *was* in my trunk. How would it have gotten there?"

"That's what the cops would like to know."

"And another thing, if the body was in *your* trunk, how is it that it was later found in the linen closet on the ninth floor?"

"We put it there. We moved it out of our trunk. After all, it wasn't our stiff, was it?"

"No. But whose was it?"

Johnny shrugged. "Lieutenant Madigan wasn't in a confiding mood — if he knew. We didn't examine him that closely. Naturally."

Walter the bartender called, "Miss Thayer, Mr. Ballinger is in the lobby. Shall I?"

"Yes, tell him to come in."

"Ken Ballinger?" Johnny asked.

"My date. You know him?"

"No, but the name sounds familiar."

Ken Ballinger came into the cocktail lounge. He was the drunk from Dinky Maguire's Pretzel Parlor. Behind him came his friend.

Ballinger was sober and did not recognize either Johnny or Sam. But the other man did.

"Ken," said Jill Thayer, "this is Mr. Fletcher and Mr. — er, Scragg. And Mr. Hale."

"Cragg," scowled Sam Cragg. "And we've met."

Harry Hale grinned at Sam Cragg. "I was hoping I'd meet you again."

"You want to make something of it?"

"Yes, but not in the way you mean. Ken, this is the lad who manhandled you."

Ken Ballinger wheeled in Sam Cragg. "I don't believe it."

"Don't mind me." Jill Thayer said drily.

"Excuse me, Jill," laughed Harry Hale. "I'll let you in on it. Ken and I were at Dinky's this afternoon and Ken, uh, I mean there was a little misunderstanding."

"I still don't believe it," Ken said sullenly. "He isn't so big."

"He's deceptive," Johnny said.

"In a peanut shell," Harry Hale cut in, "Mr. Cragg is Blockhead come to life."

Sam growled. "Lay off that Blockhead stuff. I was just looking in this magazine and — "

"Good, isn't it?" asked Harry Hale. "I'm the editor — and Ken here draws Blockhead."

Sam looked narrowly from one to the other. "Yeah? Well, look, I don't go for this. This Blockhead, he couldn't do what he does. It ain't possible. Nobody could pick up a bus in one hand."

"Couldn't you?"

"Of course not. Nobody could. And nobody could fly around in the air without an airplane."

48

"Three million readers can't be wrong."

"Eddie Miller the bellboy said the same thing," Johnny said. "This rag actually has three million paid subscribers?"

"Not paid subscribers, but buyers. It's practically all newsstand sale."

Johnny looked at Jill Thayer for confirmation. She nodded. "It's true, but don't ask me why. Blockhead has caught on and three million kids buy it every month."

"Do you work on the magazine, too?"

Jill Thayer shook her head. "Such is fame. The man never heard of me."

"Jill's the best cartoonist in the country," Ken Ballinger said. Then added, "The best woman cartoonist. She draws for the highbrow magazines. Didn't you ever see Little Cleo?"

Johnny brightened. "In *Freedom*?"

"Right!" said Harry Hale. "And what business are you in, Mr. Fletcher?"

"Me? I'm at liberty right now."

"Ah, stage?"

"Kind of."

"Good. Then this may interest you. I'd like to have Mr. Cragg give a little performance this evening."

Jill Thayer exclaimed. "But aren't you going to Boyce's party?"

"That's it, I want the boss to see something. He's always sneering about how impossible Blockhead is. I want Mr. Cragg to give a small exhibition of his strength.

"Ah," said Johnny. "Now you're talking. Sam is the strongest man in the world. Aren't you, Sam?"

"Sure, It's a small world."

Ken Ballinger cocked his head to one side, "How much do you weigh, Cragg?"

"Two hundred, or thereabouts."

"And you're not over five feet eight. I still don't believe it. I weigh a hundred and eighty myself and — "

"Stop, Ken!" cried Harry Hale. "I saw him hold you, then slap down socko."

"Sam can break a logging chain merely by his chest expansion," Johnny Fletcher said.

"Can he? I mean, could he do it tonight — at this party?"

"Well," said Johnny. "That depends."

"Of course, we expect to pay for the performance."

"How much?"

"What else can he do — in the strong arm line, I mean?"

"I'll tell you what," said Johnny. "We have a sort of act. Takes about fifteen minutes. Uh, we're a little rusty and we'd like to run through it with an audience. You promise to let us run through the complete act and it won't cost you a thing.

"I'm perfectly willing to pay. A reasonable sum, of course. Say, twenty-five dollars?"

"Mmm. Well, all right. What's the address?"

"The Bannerman on Gracie Square. I'll tell you what, we have a Blockhead costume. If Mr. Cragg could wear that during the act, it would give it a better touch — as far as we're concerned. This party is for the staff of *Blockhead*, you know. And their friends. There'll be sixty or seventy people there."

"The more the better."

"I still don't believe it," muttered Ken Ballinger.

Jill Thayer sighed. "I don't believe you were sober this afternoon either, Ken. Well, it's after eight. Don't you think we'd better get started for this brawl?"

"If I get there when the party breaks up, it's soon enough for me."

"No-no, Kenny," chided Harry Hale. "Mustn't. You promised me you'd behave."

"Oh, I will. You don't have to worry. I'll say, 'Yes, Mr. Boyce. Thank you, Mr. Boyce.'"

"Ken!" exclaimed Jill Thayer.

"Oh, all right. Come on."

"You won't disappoint us, Mr. Cragg?"

"We'll be there in a half hour. Just

get some things together. We'll see you at the brawl, all of you."

Johnny smiled pleasantly until the trio had gone, then he whirled on Sam Cragg. "We're in the money, Sam."

"I don't think he'll pay the twenty-five bucks, Johnny," Sam said. "And I don't like that business of the Blockhead uniform."

"If it amuses them, what's the difference? And don't worry about not collecting, I'll collect. Now, run and see if you can't get a box from Eddie Miller. A big carton that'll hold about forty or fifty books . . . "

"Books! Say, you're not going to — ?"

"He said he'd let us go through the act, didn't he?"

"Yeah, but — you think?"

"A man can only try," said Johnny, chuckling.

4

AND so fifteen minutes later they were in a taxicab heading for the east side and ten minutes after leaving the hotel they were climbing out in front of a tall building on the East River. A doorman looked dubiously at the big carton Sam was carrying.

"Mr. Boyce's apartment," Johnny said.

"It's the penthouse, but packages — "

"We're guests," Johnny said, sharply.

"Oh! Right this way, please."

They stepped into the elevator and were whisked to the top floor, from where they had to walk up one flight to the penthouse level. A liveried servant met them at the entrance.

"Mr. Fletcher and Mr. Cragg," Johnny said loftily.

"Can I have your things, gentlemen?"

"No, we're going to need them. Little performance we're giving."

"Thank you, sir. This way."

They walked across a stretch of graveled roof into a huge living room that was crowded with laughing, shouting, talking men and women. Harry Hale had not exaggerated in estimating the attendance to be sixty or seventy persons. There were probably closer to a hundred. And practically all were holding liquor glasses.

A man with iron-gray hair and a profile came up as they entered. "Welcome! Sorry if I don't recall the names."

"Fletcher and Cragg. Harry Hale invited us."

"Oh, Harry. You're not — "

"Yeah, Blockhead," Sam Cragg snorted.

The man sized up Sam and a little frown came to his face. "How do you do? I'm Matt Boyce, the host. Mmmmm, Harry said . . . I think he's wrong."

"He trims down good," Johnny said cheerfully.

Harry Hale dashed up. "Hello there,

Fletcher — Cragg. Ah, you've met Mr. Boyce. If you'll come with me to one of the bedrooms, I've a costume that I believe will fit Cragg. Excuse me, boss!"

As they followed Hale, Cragg muttered out of the side of his mouth. "I don't like it, Johnny."

"*I* like it," said Johnny. "I also like twenty-five bucks."

"All right, it's your funeral."

"Whose funeral?" Harry Hale asked over his shoulder. Then he pushed open a door. "This place'll do."

He entered and scowled. A man and a redheaded woman were just breaking a clinch. "Excuse me, folks."

The redhead, a very nice-looking one, patted her coiffure. "Didn't you ever learn to knock on doors, Harry?"

"My mother bought me a copy of Emily Post when I was ten," Harry Hale retorted, "but I didn't like the pictures in it. They weren't funny. I didn't know *you'd* been invited, Murphy."

"I wasn't," Murphy replied. "I'm a gatecrasher. Turnabout, you know. Boyce crashed into my business, so I'm crashing his party. Ha-ha."

"Ha-ha," Hale said, mirthlessly. "By the way, Lulu, like you to meet Blockhead, the Strong Man, Blockhead, this is *Mrs. Boyce.*"

Sam Cragg said thickly, "Look, Hale, I don't — "

Johnny Fletcher cut in, "his name is Sam Cragg, and I'm Johnny Fletcher." He winked at Mrs. Lulu Boyce. "We're going to put on a little show for the folks. Strongman stuff, you know . . . "

"Very strongman, Lulu," Hale said, sardonically. "You can feel his muscles."

"I'd love to," Lulu Boyce murmured. "Come, Danny boy."

She and Murphy left the room. Hale made a clucking sound with his mouth. "The boss's wife . . . and his deadliest enemy."

"Tsk, tsk!" said Johnny. "Well, where's this little costume of yours?"

Hale picked up a box from a dressing

table. "Here it is," he broke the string and opened the box. Sam Cragg took one look and uttered a hoarse cry of dismay.

Johnny Fletcher had the grace to whistle, but grinned crookedly.

Harry Hale look the costume out of the box. "Like it?" He held up a leopard skin.

"There ain't no one big enough to make me wear a thing like that!" Sam Cragg snarled.

"No?" Johnny went up and whispered in Sam's ear. "We now got less than six bucks between us and starvation."

Perspiration came out on Sam's forehead. "Do I . . . do I wear underwear under it?"

"Heck, no, it would show. But it's well made. Our artist's model wears it. You may find it a little tight, but . . . " Hale shrugged.

Five minutes later Sam Cragg stood with a leopard skin draped over his muscular body. It covered his torso from well above the knees to his waist, then a piece of leopard skin went over his left shoulder and down his back. A pair of sandals with leather thongs laced halfway up the calves completed the ensemble.

Sam wobbled to the mirror, cried out and reeled back. "I won't face people in this!"

"I think myself he looks kinda nice," Harry Hale said, waggishly. "The girls'll go crazy for him. Lulu Boyce especially. She likes big, strong men."

"Take the box, Sammy," Johnny said pointing to the carton they had brought with them.

Sam obeyed.

Harry Hale went to the door leading into the living room and threw it wide open.

"Ladies and gentlemen!" he cried at the top of his voice . . . "Blockhead, the Strong Man!"

The hum of conversation died for a moment, then gasps of astonishment went up as Sam Cragg slunk out of the bedroom.

"I'll take over," Johnny said to Harry Hale. He moved so his back was against the wall, then threw up his hands and roared in a voice that drowned out every other noise in the room: "Ladies and gentlemen, you all know Blockhead, the Strong Man, the strongest man in the world. Three million kids follow his adventures every month in the magazine, sixty million on television, forty million in the movies . . . and here he is in person . . . and I mean he's really Blockhead the Strong Man. He can do anything Blockhead can. Sam . . . I mean, Blockhead, the telephone directory!"

With a flick of his fingers Sam Cragg broke the heavy cord that bound the carton. He reached inside and brought out a Manhattan phone directory. He held it aloft so everyone in the room could see it, then brought it down in front of him and tore it in half almost without effort. He tossed the two sections to the floor.

"That's nothing!" howled Johnny

Fletcher. "Blockhead, the belt!"

Sam took a heavy web belt from the box. It was the sort commonly known as an army belt. Johnny took it from Sam and placed it around the latter's chest, twisting and knotting it in front.

"You think he can't break that?" Johnny asked of the audience. "There isn't another man in this room who could, but — Blockhead!"

Sam clenched his fists, let out his breath, then inhaled slowly. The belt tightened, seemed to cut into Sam's flesh, and snapped with a pop. Johnny caught it as it flew away and held up the ragged edges.

"Is there any man here who thinks he can break a similar belt? Of course there isn't. There aren't over twenty men in this entire country who could do it and none could do it with less effort than Blockhead. But that's only natural because Blockhead is the strongest man in the world. How do I know? I made him so. Look . . . "

Johnny pointed at Sam's bulging muscles, struck his chest with his fist. "You wouldn't think to look at him now that he was once a puny weakling. But he was. When he first came to me he weighed ninety-five pounds and was dying of consumption. At that time I had just learned the marvelous secrets of physical culture that have made the Aztapache Indians the strongest race in the world. I had lived among these Indians; I spoke their language and they called me brother. They confided in me. When Sam — I mean, Blockhead, came along he seemed a perfect specimen to experiment with. There was nothing to lose . . . he was dying anyway. So I applied the Aztapache principles of physical culture to him. In two weeks Blockhead's weight went up to one hundred forty pounds and he was running five miles every morning before breakfast . . . not because he had to, but because he had so much vitality. He . . . whoa, wait a *minute!*"

He turned to Sam Cragg in astonishment. "Blockhead — you can't!"

Sam had taken an inch-thick logging chain from the carton and was twisting it about his chest. "No, no, Blockhead," Johnny cried. "You can't! A horse couldn't break that chain, much less a human being. What? You say you can? No, no, even Blockhead couldn't do that. That . . . ?"

Johnny shook his head in bewilderment, then turned back to the audience. "Folks," he cried, "Blockhead insists that he can break that chain as he broke the belt. Of course you know that's impossible. No human being could do it, but . . . wouldn't it be wonderful if he could do it, if he . . . ? *Blockhead!*"

Sam had gone into a crouch. With his feet spread wide apart he came up slowly, expanding his chest. The chain cut into his flesh and Sam's face became pink, then a violet red. Perspiration broke out of his forehead.

"Don't, Blockhead!" Johnny screamed.

"You'll hurt yourself. Don't!"

And then the chain broke. It flew away from Sam and clanked to the floor with a terrific clatter. For an instant stunned silence hung over the room. It was broken by Johnny's bellow.

"*He did it!* He broke a chain that a horse couldn't break. He did it. Do you believe now that he's the strongest man in the world? Are you convinced now that these Aztapache physical culture secrets are the real McCoy? Are there any men here who are weak, sickly, rundown. Anyone who would like to become strong? Don't despair . . . *you can be!* I've got it all here. I didn't think it was right to keep this secret from the world, so I had it written up. The simple, secret exercises that turned Blockhead from a ninety-five pound weakling into the strongest man in the world. It's all here in this book." Timing it nicely Sam Cragg had delved into the paper carton and brought forth an armful of *Every Man a Samson*. He tossed one copy to Johnny, who caught it and waved it over his head.

"It's all here in this astounding book, *Every Man a Samson*. I'm going to let every man here have a copy and I'm not going to charge fifty dollars for it, nor even twenty-five or fifteen and heaven knows it's worth ten times that. No, I'm going to pass out these wonderful little books for the puny, paltry, insignificant sum of three dollars and ninety-five cents . . . and here I come!"

"Mr. Fletcher!" cried Harry Hale, in horror. "You can't — "

Johnny grabbed an armful of books and brushed Harry Hale to one side. "Here you are, sir, the book that'll make you as strong as Blockhead. Thank you. Four dollars . . . five cents tax, makes it come out even. And you, sir? The little lady likes strong men. Miss, feel Blockhead's muscles."

The girl did . . . and so did a number of others as Sam followed Johnny through the crowd passing out books. The place was in an uproar, laughter prevailing and punctuated by Johnny Fletcher's booming voice as he exhorted men to buy copies of *Every Man a Samson*. Harry Hale caught up with him once more, but still Johnny ignored him.

Then finally Johnny brought up face to face with the host, Matt Boyce. "I suppose Harry Hale put you up to this?" Boyce demanded, his face flushed in anger.

"Hale? No. It's my own idea. You'd like a copy?"

"No! But come to my office tomorrow morning."

"Sure, how about you, sir?"

"Pfft!" said Lieutenant Madigan of Homicide.

Johnny winced. He had not seen Madigan come in. "Crashing the party?"

"Yeah, and you? A very good pitch. I haven't heard better on Forty-second Street."

"That's because I've been out of town. What's new?"

Lieutenant Madigan looked steadily at Sam Cragg. "You look natural in that pussycat skin."

Sam bared his teeth. "What I do to make a buck!"

Madigan chuckled and turned back to Johnny. "Where's the boss of this layout?"

"Right over there, the gent with the profile. Business with him?"

"And maybe you, too." Lieutenant Madigan went over to Matt Boyce. "Mr. Boyce, could I have a few minutes? I'm Lieutenant Madigan of Homicide."

Boyce looked from Madigan to Fletcher. "Homicide?"

"Yes. Do you know a man named Hal Soderstrom?"

"Yes, why . . . ?"

"That's what I'd like to talk to you about."

"Homicide Squad . . . you mean . . . ?"

"Yes. Is there somewhere we can go?"

"Yes. Come along."

67

Madigan signaled to Johnny Fletcher, "You, too."

"Okay, we've about finished here anyway."

Sam was so willing to leave the crowded room that he ran ahead of the others to the bedroom and was already putting on his shirt when they entered.

Once the door was closed, Matt Boyce nodded pointedly at Johnny. "What about them?"

"They're in this. You might call them suspects."

"Ixnay, Madigan," exclaimed Johnny. "There's such a thing as libel."

"Sue me. Mr. Boyce, I understand Hal Soderstrom was an employee of yours."

"That's right, but I — I can't believe he's dead. I saw him only yesterday. And murdered . . . !"

"He was found in a linen closet of the 45th Street Hotel, his head bashed in with a blunt instrument. There were no identifying papers on his person, which is why it took several hours for us to identify him."

"How'd you finally do it?"

"Fingerprints. They were on file."

Boyce looked sharply at Madigan. "Eh?"

"He'd served time in Sing Sing. Didn't you know that?"

"Good lord, no! What — what for?"

Madigan pursed his lips. "Blackmail. Three years."

Boyce shook his head in bewilderment. "I hadn't the slightest idea. He worked for me four years or more . . . "

"And was he a good employee?"

"Absolutely. Well, I mean he'd have a hangover now and then on a Monday, but I don't hold that against a man. I like a drink myself."

"In what capacity did he work for you?"

"Why, he was the business manager of *Blockhead*."

"Blockhead? What . . . " Madigan's eyes went suddenly to Sam Cragg, who was almost fully dressed. "Say

— that costume looked familiar. Sure, Blockhead. I get it now." His face twitched and he suddenly began to chuckle. "Sam Cragg Blockhead."

"You think it's funny?" Sam sneered.

"If I'd had a camera I'd taken a picture of you in that costume and got rich selling prints at Coney Island."

"And you're a reader of *Blockhead*," Johnny cut in sarcastically.

That brought Madigan back to business. He said to Boyce, "I understand you're the publisher of *Blockhead*."

"That's right. I'm president of the Boyce Publishing Company. But I assure you Soderstrom's death had nothing to do with the affairs of the company. And I still don't see how these men have any connection with Soderstrom."

"I don't see myself. But there's a peculiar coincidence that touches them. There was blood on Sodertrom's hand and the hand had touched a book so that part of the title left its imprint on the hand. The complete title of the

70

book is *Every Man a Samson* and these men are salesmen for it . . . "

"What?" Boyce looked sharply at Johnny. "That was a real sales talk out there? Hale knew what you were and — "

"No," Johnny said. "He didn't know. He wanted to hire Sam to play Blockhead; promised to pay twenty-five dollars. I told him we had a regular strongman act and he said to put it on. Well, we did. Mmm, maybe I forgot to tell Hale that part of the act consisted of selling books at the end of the pitch."

"You *forgot*," Madigan exclaimed. "I'll bet you forgot to tell him! Just one of your little stunts."

"You seem to know these men, Lieutenant?"

Madigan snorted. "Too well. I know — "

"Now, now, Lieutenant," Johnny chided. "Didn't I solve a case for you once? Is that the thanks I get?"

Madigan scratched his ear. "The

devil of it, Mr. Boyce, is that he's telling the truth. He did *help* with a case once . . . but he was mixed up in it as deep as he is on this one."

"And the case was just as tough!" Johnny winked at Madigan. "If you asked me nice, I might help you with this one."

"No, thanks. Me and the police department will struggle along without your help. Unless, of course, you want to tell me how the imprint from that book got on Sodertsrom's hand."

"I would if I could."

"Well," said Matt Boyce. "What can I tell you about Soderstrom?"

"Everything there is to tell. Was he married?"

"Not in recent years. I understand he was divorced eight or ten years ago. He never spoke of his past, come to think of it. He started with me as an advertising salesman and when I launched *Blockhead* — "

"You published other magazines before *Blockhead*?"

"Yes, I've been in the publishing business fifteen years."

"What magazines?"

Boyce made a deprecating gesture. "Nothing important. Some, uh, cats and dogs. *Blockhead* is the most successful magazine I have. And I don't mind saying that no small part of its success was due to Hal Soderstrom. I'm going to miss him."

"Of course. But you haven't really told me anything about him yet. He must have had some enemies, one at least."

5

BEFORE Boyce could reply to that, there was knock on the door and Harry Hale peeked in. When he saw Sam Cragg was fully dressed he said, "Okay" over his shoulder and came in. Jill Thayer followed.

"Hi, boss," Hale said, breezily. "What'd you think of Blockhead?"

"I'll talk to you about that tomorrow."

"It was a magnificent performance," said Jill Thayer. "Especially Mr. Fletcher's."

Johnny chuckled. "Thank you kindly. Mr. Hale, there's a little matter . . . you know, the remuneration."

"What? Why, you must have taken at least a hundred dollars."

"Maybe so, but you said you'd pay twenty-five dollars."

"Wearing the caveman outfit was

worth twenty-five bucks," Sam Cragg groused.

"Please," Interrupted Matt Boyce. "There are more important things. This is Lieutenant Madigan of the police department. Mr. Hale, editor of *Blockhead* and — excuse me — Miss Thayer, a famous cartoonist. Harry, the lieutenant brought some shocking information; Hal Soderstrom is dead."

"Hal?" cried Harry Hale. "No wonder he didn't show up tonight. Bad whiskey?"

"A blunt instrument," said Johnny Fletcher.

Lieutenant Madigan stepped forward. "You can go, Fletcher. I know where to reach you, in case."

"Oh, I don't mind sticking around if I can help . . ."

"You can't. In four syllable words, beat it!"

"You mean you want me to go? All right, if that's what you want." With an injured air Johnny gestured to Jill Thayer. "I'll take you home."

Jill started to shake her head, then suddenly followed Johnny and Sam out of the room. Just outside the door Sam picked up the carton that had contained the books. "Some dirty crooks swiped the books that we left over. There must have been six or eight . . ."

"S'tough," said Johnny. "Look, Jill. I rescued you. This Soderstrom is the lad who was in your trunk this afternoon."

"That's a lie," Jill declared hotly. "I scarcely knew the man."

"Oh, you did know him?"

"Slightly, I said. Since he was nominally Ken's superior at the office I heard his name mentioned now and then. And I met him once or twice."

"By the way, where *is* the boy friend?"

Jill shrugged a well-moulded shoulder. "Where's the bar?"

"Oh! Maybe you'd better let me take you home after all."

"I know the way. To be frank, Mr.

Fletcher, I don't care an awful lot for you."

"That's because you don't know me well. Let me tell you about myself and — "

"Write me a letter, and don't put a stamp on the envelope."

Johnny grimaced. "We're getting nowhere fast. Well, I guess I'll have to confess to lieutenant, after all."

"Confess?"

"Tell the truth. How I found the body . . . why we moved it . . . you know."

"Now don't try anything like that. I hate blackmail in any shape, form or variety."

"Shh!" said Johnny. "People will hear you."

"Johnny," said Sam, "here comes trouble!"

Ken Ballinger was weaving drunkenly through the crowd. A stocky young blond in a tuxedo was trying to hold him back but wasn't having very good success.

Ken came up to Sam Cragg and glared owlishly at him. "I saw it and I still don't believe it. That chain was a phony."

"Sure," said Sam, easily. "So was the telephone book."

"Ken!" exclaimed Jill. "You're drunk again."

"I am like ducks. This ginzo hit me when I wasn't looking this afternoon and I owe him something."

Sam yawned. "Come around some-time when you grow up."

"You . . . !" said Ken, thickly. He made a sudden swing for Sam's face. The latter ducked it easily, reached out and wrapped his arms about Ken. He picked him up and stooping low laid Ken across his knees. Then holding him securely with one hand he administered something Ken Ballinger had probably not had for twenty years — an old-fashioned spanking. And he didn't spare him.

The whacks across the seat of the trousers made considerable noise and before Sam finished half the people in the room were watching. Then Sam lifted Ken to his feet and pushed him against the wall.

Ken, sobbing from either pain or drunken rage, swung wildly with both fists, but none of the blows landed.

"Let it go, Sammy," Johnny ordered sharply.

"Okay," said Sam and stepped back swiftly. Ken fell forward on his face. Jill brushed past Johnny Fletcher and dropped to her knees. She turned up her face and it was white with suppressed anger.

"I think you'd better go," she said. "And take your — your gorilla with you."

"That's you, Sam," said Johnny, cheerfully. "Come on."

Silently people gave way and made a lane. As they reached the door, someone called to Johnny. "Say!"

He turned. It was the stocky blond. "I just wanted to say that it was Ken's fault. He's been looking for trouble all day. He left the office at noon with a chip on his shoulder." The blond head nodded. "Like to have you come to the office tomorrow. Want to talk to you about modeling."

"No," Sam Cragg snapped.

"You mean because of Ken? He'll be over it by tomorrow. *Blockhead* can afford to pay for a good model. Give me a buzz. My name's Jim Wilder."

"We may do that little thing," said Johnny.

As they descended the flight of stairs to the twentieth floor, Sam Cragg muttered, "Next guy mentions Blockhead to me gets a poke in the nose. I was never so humiliated in my life."

Johnny chuckled. "But I sold thirty-two books. That's one hundred twenty-eight dollars. Not bad for an evening's work."

Sam sighed. "Some time I'm going to get heart failure the stuff you pull. I thought sure we'd get kicked out."

"Well, we did finally. But that was

because of your rough stuff."

"With that Ken? He couldn't take a hint."

"Maybe he'll try for you again tomorrow. He lives at the hotel, you know. Mmm, so does the Jill girl. A very nice number."

"Huh? Say, you're not falling . . ."

"Me? scoffed Johnny. "Do I ever fall for dames?"

"Yes!"

The elevator door opened and Johnny was spared replying to that. Outside he signaled a cab and when they were in began talking about trivial things.

It was after eleven when they reached the hotel. Mr. Peabody was behind the desk, filing his fingernails. He held up his hand as Johnny and Sam started toward the elevator.

"Mr. Fletcher, I've been thinking about all this and I've decided to insist upon the house rules being followed to the exact spirit, rather than the letter."

"What does that mean in English?"

"Your personal property isn't worth five dollars. A couple of shirts, some socks . . . "

"You been snooping in our room?" Johnny snapped.

"I have a right, Mr. Fletcher. As manager of this hotel."

"Look," said Johnny, "I'm getting awfully tired of you asking for the room rent, so . . . " Johnny pulled a handful of crumpled bills from his pocket, " . . . I'm going to pay that week's rent in advance. Twenty-five dollars."

Mr. Peabody's eyes threatened to bulge from his head as he stared at the money. Johnny chuckled wickedly. "I'll bet you thought I didn't have the money and you expected to stick a French key into our lock. Eh? Well, there it is — and a receipt, if you please. You don't trust me; I don't trust you. So we understand each other."

Mr. Peabody wrote out a receipt, but he was not happy about it.

Johnny and Sam rode up to the eighth floor. The moment they entered their room, Johnny went to the telephone. "Hello, operator," he said. "I'd like to have a pitcher of ice water . . . and have Eddie Miller bring it. Thank you!"

He hung up to meet Sam's frowning face. "Ice water, Johnny?"

"I'm thirsty."

"I could do with a cold bottle of beer."

"Ice water will be better for you. I don't want you to get woozy."

"After the evening I've had I'm entitled to something," Sam said crossly.

"The evening isn't over yet."

"What do you mean, Johnny?" There was alarm in Sam's tone. "You're not going to . . . stick out your neck again?"

There was a soft tapping on the door and Eddie Miller's voice came through the panels. "Ice water, Mr. Fletcher."

"Come in!"

Eddie came in carrying a pitcher. "Ice water, Mr. Fletcher?" he asked, with his tongue in his cheek.

"Ice water, Eddie," Johnny smiled pleasantly and took the handful of bills from his pocket. Eddie Miller stared, fascinated. Johnny disengaged a dollar bill, examined it and added another.

He handed the money to Eddie. "You're a good kid, Eddie. I like you."

Eddie stowed the bills in his pockets. "You musta hit the jackpot, Mr. Fletcher."

"I did, practically. And I'm going to keep on hitting it now . . . "

"Two bucks for ice water!" Sam exploded.

"Tsk, tsk, tsk, Sam," Johnny chided. "Eddie knows it isn't for the ice water! It's just because he's done us some turns at times and I want to show my appreciation."

"Gee, thanks, Mr. Fletcher. Any time I can do anything for you . . . "

"As a matter of fact, Eddie, you could do me a little favor right now."

"Oh-oh! What is it?"

"Oh, I guess it isn't important. Skip

it, Eddie. You might get in a jam and I wouldn't want you to lose your job. *You* know I wouldn't really touch anything, but if that boss of yours got wind he'd say I was robbing the room . . . "

"A room, Mr. Fletcher?"

"Yeah, I thought I'd like to take a quick peek into a room. I've got a little clue I'd like to investigate."

"A clue? You're working on the murder case? Cripes, that sounds interesting, but . . . ah, what room was you wanting to look into?"

"Oh, it doesn't matter. You couldn't get the key for me anyway, could you?"

"The key? Well, uh, mm, you see, I got a passkey. Fits any door in the house. Uh, just a key I happened to have and one day I discovered it was a duplicate of the house passkey . . . "

"Of course, Eddie. I understand. You wouldn't deliberately swipe the house passkey and have a duplicate made . . . Mmm, let's see this key, Eddie."

Eddie took it from his pocket. "What room you figuring on looking into."

"The one right above this; it's right next to the linen closet where they, well, you know."

"Yeah, sure. I looked it up. Room 921's occupied by a bird named Holcomb. The register says he's from Terra Haute, Indiana, and he might be at that. An old geezer. But look, Mr. Fletcher, you'll be . . . uh careful?"

"I give you my word and I'm not going to forget this little favor. And thanks for the ice water!"

"You're welcome, Mr. Fletcher."

Eddie Miller frowned and hesitated, but Johnny gave him no encouragement and the bellboy reluctantly left the room. Johnny put his finger to his lips and waited a couple of minutes. Then he went to the door and peered out cautiously.

"You'd better stay here, Sam. I'll be back in ten minutes."

"I'll be holding my breath."

Johnny winked and slipped out of

the room. But instead of climbing on the ninth floor he went quickly down the seventh and approached the door of Room 721. A peek through the keyhole showed him that the room was dark and he unlocked the door and went in. He locked the door on the inside, then switched on the light.

The trunk still stood in the corner. Johnny went to it and lifted the lid. The trunk was empty. He leaned far into it and struck a match. By its light he examined the interior closely. He exclaimed in chagrin. The bottom of the trunk was wet to his touch. It had been washed thoroughly and the water soaking into the lining had not yet dried out completely.

"So she didn't know," he muttered. He closed the trunk and went to the clothes closet. It was full of clothing and a drawing stand on which was screwed a drawing board. There was a rough pencil sketch tacked on the board — a caricature, but Johnny's eyes traveled back to it after passing it once.

He chuckled. It was a caricature of himself, his features made angular, his nose more prominent than it actually was. But quite recognizable. With a mere curved line or two, Jill Thayer had put a bold look into the caricature's eyes that gave the impression that Johnny was pretty much a sly wolf.

He closed the closet door and went to the chiffonier. For the first time he noticed now that the furnishings were not an exact duplicate of those in his own room. Beside the chiffonier stood a cabinet. He opened it and discovered that most of Jill's drawing supplies were here, There were stacks of pencil and drybrush drawings, even a few in crayon. There was also a huge stack of magazines. Johnny took one out and began leafing through it. After a moment he came upon a printed cartoon, signed Jill Thayer. It was a good cartoon and produced a chuckle from Johnny. The magazine was a large circulation weekly.

He moved from the cabinet to the

hotel desk and noted that a portable typewriter in its case stood underneath.

He pulled upon the large drawer of the desk and exclaimed as he saw a packet of letters, held together with a thick rubber band. He scooped up the bundle and then a click behind him caused him to whirl guiltily.

He winced as he saw the door opening. But the person who came into the room holding a key was not the one he had expected.

It was a man, a tall slender young man of about twenty-five. He was as astonished to see Johnny as the latter was to see the masculine intruder.

"What the . . . !" the man exclaimed.

"You've got the wrong room, mister," Johnny said quickly. Behind his back he dropped the packet of letters into the open desk drawer.

The newcomer blinked, then shot a quick glance at the number on the door just a few inches from his face. A scowl came to his face.

"*You've* got the wrong room. What

the devil are you doing here?"

"What?" exclaimed Johnny. "I guess I ought to know my own room. I checked in this afternoon. See!" He thrust his hand into his pocket and brought out the key of Room 821. He held up the tag. "Room 821, see?"

"This is Room 721."

"You're crazy," Johnny cried.

The other tapped the door. "Look for yourself."

Johnny went forward and peered at the door. "Well, I'll be damned! It *is* 821. But jeez, it's exactly like my own room and I even have a trunk like that one. I'll be a monkey's uncle. *Excuse me*, Mister. I was out to a movie and just came in. The elevator man left me off a floor too soon, and I stepped into *your* room."

The man at the door did not rise to that bait. He grunted and stepped to one side so Johnny could walk past him. But Johnny lingered. "This one of those embarrassing moments, I guess, Mister . . . er . . . ? by the way, my name's Fletcher."

"So?"

"Nothing. Cripes, you about scared the life out of me, coming in like that. I'm kinda skittish anyway. You know . . . what happened in the hotel today." He paused. "The murder, I mean."

"Things happen in hotels right along. Goodnight."

"Good night," said Johnny. "And . . . sorry."

"G'night!"

Johnny left and climbed halfway up to the eighth floor. Then he paused. It was a long minute before the door of Room 721 finally closed and then Johnny heard footsteps slither in the hall carpeting. The man had come out of Room 721 was going away from the room, down the hall, past the elevators.

Johnny tiptoed quickly to the seventh floor level and crouching peered into the hallway. At the end, where a short hall led to the right from the main corridor, the young man stopped at a door and began putting a key into the lock. He unlocked the door and went in.

Johnny counted up to fifty, then stepped into the corridor and walked as softly as he could, until he could see the number on the door. It was 717. He nodded and, turning, headed back for the stairs.

He encountered Sam Cragg in the upper corridor, as jittery as a cat with nine kittens. "Gee, Johnny!" he breathed hoarsely.

Johnny went into their room and Sam followed. "You were gone fifteen minutes, Johnny."

Johnny shook his head sadly. "I've learned something and it hurts."

"Huh?"

"I've learned," Johnny said, "That the more beautiful they are the more they lie."

6

THE sun shining on Johnny Fletcher's face wakened him in the morning. He rolled over lazily and looked out of the window to the roof of the adjoining building, which came just the level of the eighth floor of the 45th Street Hotel.

A fat woman was hanging out washing on the roof. Such early morning energy on the part of others almost made him uncomfortable. He got out of bed and pulled down the window shade, then went to the telephone stand between the beds and looked at the cheap watch that was ticking noisily. It was eight-thirty.

Johnny exclaimed and slapped Sam Cragg. Sam grunted and pulled the blanket higher over his head. Johnny hit him again.

"Rise and shine, Blockhead!" Sam

threw back the blanket. "Who said that?" he snarled, then opened his eyes and recognized Johnny. "What's the matter?"

"Up! This is a new day and there are things to do. The things we should have done yesterday."

Sam groaned. "I thought I was just having a nightmare, but now I remember. I wish it had been a nightmare."

Johnny chuckled and went into the bathroom. He took a shower and when he came out Eddie Miler was knocking on the door. "Telegram, Mr. Fletcher!"

"Collect or prepaid?"

Eddie Miller mumbled an unintelligible reply, but Johnny opened the door and let him in. His hands were empty.

"I just said telegram in case anyone was prowling around," Eddie grinned. "I just came to get the key."

"What key?"

"You know, the passkey?"

"You mean you carry around a

passkey to all the rooms? It is customary for bellboys in hotels to have one?"

"Aw, cut it out, Mr. Fletcher. I took a chance letting you have it."

"Okay, Eddie. Here it is. But tell me something. What's the name of the party in Room 717?"

"Seven seventeen? Umm, isn't that a tall, young fellow about twenty-five?"

"That's right. Who is he?"

"Name's Johnson. Thomas Johnson. He's down on the book as coming from Iowa. I forget the name of the town. Some whistlestop like Shell Rock or Shell Creek. Why are you interested in him?"

"Why are *you* interested in him? Or do you check up on all the guests?"

"Just the permanent. Johnson's been here two weeks and don't seem to be doing much of anything. He's around most of the time. You know what that means?"

"What?"

"He'll fall a week behind in his rent, then another. And Peabody will slip him the French key — lock him out."

"Hasn't he got any friends?"

"I haven't seem him with any. He goes out every day for a couple of hours, but most of the time he just stays here in his room. Don't seem natural for a guy from Iowa, in the big town. But look, Mr. Fletcher, you're barking up the wrong tree if you're connecting him with the guy who was bumped here yesterday."

"Oh, I wasn't interested in him in that connection at all."

"No?"

"No, Eddie. Thanks a lot for the use of your key."

"You're welcome. Peabody . . . "

Eddie stopped as a pile driver smashed repeatedly against the thin panels of the door.

"Wake up Fletcher!" boomed the voice of Lieutenant Madigan.

Johnny groaned. "Before breakfast! Come in flatfoot!"

Lieutenant Madigan slammed open the door and sidestepped Eddie

Miller's swift exit.

"Hi, Fletcher," Madigan said, in great humor. "And Blockhead!"

"I punched a cop in the nose for calling me less than that," Sam Cragg snapped.

"I'm trembling, Cragg. I may take you up on that, down at Headquarters some time."

"I had a goodnight's sleep, Madigan," Johnny said, "and now I'm hungry. So cut short whatever nonsense brought you here."

"The taxpayers don't think murder is nonsense. I thought I'd come in and give you a chance to spill whatever's on your mind."

"There's nothing on my mind, Madigan." Johnny gave the detective a suspicious glance. "Why should there be?"

"Oh, I was just putting some coincidences together, that's all. The coincidence of the title of one of your books being on Hal Soderstrom's hand. And you showing up at the Boyce party."

97

"We were hired to put on a show."

"By Harry Hale? When did he hire you?"

"Before the party — naturally. As a matter of fact, we had a little brush with Harry Hale and Ken Ballinger in the afternoon. We stopped in at Dinky Maguire's up the street for a glass of beer and Ken was crying in his beer. He thought Sam shoved him off and Hale got the idea that Sam had some moxie so later when we met him he made that proposition."

"Where did this 'later' take place?"

"Down in the cocktail lounge."

"Who was present?"

"Me and Sam, Harry Hale and Ken Ballinger."

"Anyone else?"

Johnny frowned. "Jill Thayer, the cartoonist."

"Ah, yes, she lives here at the hotel."

"So does Ken Ballinger."

"That's right. Ballinger introduced you to Miss Thayer, I suppose?"

"What're you trying to do, Madigan?"

Johnny snapped testily. "You pumped that whole crew last night; now you're springing stuff on me, trying to catch me. No, Ballinger didn't introduce me to the girl. I met her here at the hotel."

"How?"

"Am I sixty-seven years old? Have I got false teeth and a wig? Is Jill Thayer an old hag? I got off the wrong floor one time and thought her room was this one . . . "

"What do you mean, one time? You only checked in here yesterday."

"It was yesterday that happened."

"And before evening you were having a drink with her in the cocktail lounge."

"The place has a license to sell drinks."

"So it has. Mind if I do some thinking out loud, Fletcher?"

"Yes. I mind. I mind your busting in here, but it doesn't do me any good, does it?"

"No. So I'll just talk. This Hal

Soderstrom was business manager of *Blockhead, the Strong Man*, a very cushy job, I understand. So he comes here to the 45th Street Hotel and gets his head bashed in and is stuffed into a linen closet, right above the room in which you're holing up. On his hand was a reverse printing of the title of a book you keep in your trunk . . . but you deny that the body was ever near one of your books."

"Have you got the book to prove it was?"

"Yes."

"What?"

Lieutenant Madigan whistled. The door of the room opened and Detective Fox came in. He carried a small newspaper-wrapped parcel. One look at it and a shudder shook Johnny.

Lieutenant Madigan gave him a cat-and-mouse look. "Know what's in the package, Fletcher?"

"No-no . . . "

"Open it, Foxie!"

Detective Fox removed the newspaper

from the package, revealing a towel. He unfolded the towel carefully and finally exposed three copies of *Every Man a Samson*. He handled them gingerly by the edges.

"You never saw these before?" Madigan asked. "I got them down in the checkroom. I got to thinking what I would do if I was stuck with something like that . . . and I figured I'd check the package for a few days. So I stopped at the checkroom on my way in and sure enough there was a package there, checked by Mr. Fletcher of Room 821."

"It's a lie," Johnny said hoarsely. "I didn't check that package."

"There's some fingerprints on the book," Detective Fox said.

"Fine, Foxie," purred Madigan. "That's just fine. If they match up with Mr. Fletcher, I think, mmm, we may have a little room down at Headquarters."

7

JOHNNY FLETCHER worried his lower lip with his teeth. Then suddenly he sighed in surrender. "Okay, Madigan. I'll talk."

"I'm not making any promises," the detective said, sharply.

"You don't have to. You know damn well I didn't kill Soderstrom. We checked into this room yesterday afternoon at two o'clock. We came here straight from the bus station. The express company had already delivered our trunk and we had it brought up here. So then we washed up and went out to see Mort Murray, the guy from whom we buy our books. We got back here about five o'clock and Sam opened the trunk. Soderstrom was in it . . . "

"At five o'clock?"

"A few minutes before five. Well, you can imagine how we felt, opening our trunk and finding a stiff in it."

"I had nightmares last night," Sam Cragg said.

"I'm having them now," Madigan said, drily. "Go on, Fletcher. What then?"

"We didn't know what to do — so we went out to have a drink. That's when we had the brush with Ken Ballinger and Harry Hale. So then we came back — and took the body up to the linen closet on the ninth floor."

"And when'd you meet this girl?"

Johnny cleared his throat. "Uh, then. I was going to put the body on the seventh floor and went ahead to see if the Coast was clear. Jill's door was open so I had Sam take the body up to the ninth floor instead."

"I see. Now just one thing more. I tumbled to the book trick. You wouldn't let me break open the lock of the trunk, because you hadn't checked over the books. You did that while I was getting the locksmith. But Foxie was outside your door while I was gone

— so you didn't get the books out then. Where were they when I looked for them?"

"At the end of a string hanging outside the window."

Lieutenant Madigan snorted. "You know what I think, Fletcher? That you're the biggest liar I ever threw in the clink."

"Every word I told you is the truth."

"Yeah! There's only one thing saves you — and I'll bet you don't even know what it is."

"I'm all ears."

"It's the time element. I checked on the register downstairs. You did check in at two-ten. And Doc Ryerson swears that Soderstrom was killed at least three hours before that time — around eleven. And that makes the problem even tougher."

Johnny whistled softly. "You mean . . . ?"

"Where was the body between eleven and two? Your trunk came to the hotel yesterday morning. They held it downstairs until you checked in, so the body couldn't have been put in *before two*. But where was it since eleven?"

Johnny shook his head slowly. "You gave me an alibi yourself."

"I know it, dammit. I even checked at the bus station on Forty-fourth Street. You came in on the one fifty-five bus. The driver remembers you, since he had you ever since Cleveland and you made yourselves conspicuous enough on the bus. But where was Soderstrom from eleven until two?"

"That," said Johnny, "is the mystery."

"You're telling me? It's driving me crazy." Madigan scowled. "Ballinger's got a hole up on the eleventh floor and he's got an alibi from three o'clock on. Dinky Maguire's . . . "

"And before three?"

"I'm checking the rest of it. He went down to the office, half-crocked, and Harry Hale sent him home."

"And Hale?"

"Ballinger telephoned him from some dump on Sixth Avenue and Hale went to pick him up. That was around eleven. Both claim they started walking toward the hotel. They stopped at three or four places before they got to Dinky MagThen theuire's. It's a lousy alibi for both of them, but it's the best I can do until I break it down with a stop watch."

"What about Matt Boyce, Soderstrom's boss?"

Madigan turned up his palms and shrugged. "As smooth as they come. The big club and businessman. He got up at ten o'clock, walked over to the club and had a little workout, then strolled to business — along about noon. Phooey!"

Johnny Fletcher pursed his lips and regarded Madigan thoughtfully for a moment. Then he nodded as if reaching a decision.

"Look, Maddy, no use your holding this against me. Or me being sore at you. I like you, so I'll give you a tip. Last night, at Boyce's, we burst in on a guy who was in a clinch with Matt Boyce's wife. Fella name of Murphy.

106

He made a crack about Boyce muscling in on his business and him muscling in on Boyce's wife . . . "

"I've got a record of Murphy," said Madigan. "It was given me by — someone."

"Yeah? Well, who — and what — is he?"

"He's an ex-publisher — hey, who's asking the questions here."

"You."

"All right, then, let *me* ask them. How'd you get acquainted with Jill Thayer?"

"You want to learn my technique, Maddy? I generally charge for that, but seeing how it's *you*, I'll tell you. I use the subtle, indirect approach; for instance I see a good-looking dame, I march up to her and say, 'Look, babe, how's about you and me stepping out?'"

Lieutenant Madigan suddenly had difficulty with his breathing. "Fletcher," he said, thickly, "some day you're going to get me sore . . . "

"Oh, I wouldn't want to do *that*!"

"Ah-r-r!" Madigan choked and stamped out of the room. Johnny winked at Sam Cragg.

"That worked pretty neatly."

Sam sniffed. "By the skin of your teeth. This time. What do you say we check the whole thing?"

"I'm willing. How about a good breakfast and then a trip down to Mort Murray?"

"Mort? Uh, you know what he said yesterday . . . ?"

"Yeah, but he didn't really mean that. We only owe him a hundred and fifty dollars. Mort'd starve without us and he knows it. We've only got a few books left; hardly enough to make a pitch. Mm, I may give him a few dollars on accounts. A few."

They left the hotel, then walked to Broadway where they had breakfast at the Automat. Then they took the subway to Eighteenth Street and walked two blocks to Mort Murray's office on West Sixteenth. It was on the fourth floor of an ancient loft building and consisted of two rooms, one of which Mort used as a storeroom. There was a sign on the door, *Murray Publishing Company*, but that didn't mean anything because Murray wasn't actually a publisher. He operated a mail order business selling books to salesmen. He handled only the one title, *Every Man a Samson*, which he bought from the actual publisher in quantity and resold to salesmen.

He was a lean, slender young man in his early thirties, with unruly black hair. He was reading *Racing Form* when Johnny and Sam stepped into his office, but leaped up when he saw them.

"Hi, fellows! I was just thinking about you."

"Did you see our names in that *Racing Form*?"

Mort coughed. "As a matter of fact there's a good nag in the fourth at Aqueduct and I was thinking if I had some dough I'd put a sawbuck on him.

109

The plug can't lose. He practically told me so himself."

"Speaking of money, Mort, that's why we came here. To slip you some. We had a good day yesterday and — "

Mort got very pale. "Money — you came here to give me money?"

"Yeah, sure. Why not? What're the odds on this nag?"

"Twenty to one, but he's a cinch, I tell you. They got him doped wrong — "

"They do that sometimes, don't they? Well, if you're so sure of it, here take this and put it on his nose — "

He handed a couple of bills to Mort. The latter looked at them and cried out hoarsely. "That's only two bucks!"

"It'll earn you forty, won't it?"

Mort Murray grabbed his desk to steady himself. Tears came to his eyes. "Why do you do these things to me, Johnny? I've got a weak heart. First, you talk about giving me a wad on account and then you slip me two bucks."

"Don't you want it? I'm not so well heeled I can't use it myself. I thought in view of your having such a good thing in that race . . . "

Mort snatched the bills from Johnny's hand. "Cut it out, Johnny. Go away and let me suffer in silence."

"Well, if that's the way you feel about it, after all the business I've thrown you in the past . . . "

"Sure, Johnny. No need to get sore. You're the best customer I've got. One year you bought ten thousand books from me — but that was six years ago."

"And I'm going to make a comeback. Things are ripe and I'm feeling better than I ever felt in my life."

"Don't you believe it, Mort," Sam Cragg cut in sarcastically. "We're playing detective again. You know what that means; I get the hell knocked out of me and we wind up without a dime."

"What mess are you in now?"

"Didn't you read in the papers last

night about the guy who was found in a linen closet at the 45th Street Hotel?"

"Yeah, sure, and I knew you were at that joint. I guess I should have known you were mixed up in it. What's the lowdown?"

"That's the exact word, Mort. Some lowdown so-and-so pulled a low down trick on us and stuffed that corpse in our trunk. *We* put it in the linen closet."

"*I* did," Sam corrected.

"Same thing. Well, you read about this guy being in the publishing business, Mort. That's what I thought I'd ask you about — you being in the same racket. What d'you know about Soderstrom?"

"Nothing, but I've heard of Matt Boyce. They say he's a card."

"How do you mean?"

"Oh, he's knocked around the fringes of the publishing business for a good many years — and never had a legitimate magazine until he robbed *Blockhead* from Dan Murphy."

"Hey," said Sam Cragg, "Murphy's the name of the guy who was necking with the redhead."

"You've got a memory like an elephant, Sammy," Johnny Fletcher said drily. "So Boyce swiped the magazine from Murphy. How?"

"How should I know? Those things never get out. Murphy owned the magazine, or was supposed to own it, then all of a sudden Matt Boyce took it over — just when it started clicking."

"Maybe Boyce really owned it right along?"

"Could be. I don't know. But he never owned anything decent before. They say he was selling hot dogs at Coney Island eighteen years ago. And I know he was interested in some horse dope sheets. Then a couple of years ago he broke out with *Blockhead* and made a million bucks . . . Maybe I don't live right. Nothing like that ever happens to me."

"Lightning may strike you yet — if

you keep out in the rain. Mmm, ever hear of Hal Soderstrom?"

"Isn't that the name of the guy who got bumped?"

"That's him."

Mort Murray shook his head. "I never heard his name until this."

"He did time for blackmail."

"Even so I never heard of him. But I'm not surprised if he's mixed up with Matt Boyce."

"How come? Matt go in for the slip-it-to-me-or-else?"

Mort shrugged. "Do you remember a blackmail sheet that was published in town some years ago called *Town Trumpet*? There was a rumor once that Boyce was the guy behind it; but the cops got a dope named Egbert Craddock."

"What'd they do to him?"

"Sent him up. I remember reading about it in the papers."

"The charge was blackmail, eh? Just how did this rag operate?"

"Oh, it was very fancy. The magazine

circulated among the smart set and ran articles and stuff on fox-hunting and how to drink tea out of a saucer. Then it had a department, which it called *Eavesdropping*. That's where the dynamite was. The editor would send an advance proof of *Eavesdropping* to Joe Dough, with a note saying, 'We thought you might be interested in seeing this advance proof which goes to press the day after tomorrow.' Joe Dough would look it over and see a little item, like: 'Joe Dough is one employer who treats his help swell. Because his secretary had to work overtime so much, Joe bought her a nifty mink coat, to keep her warm while going home.' So Joe, knowing that his wife would read that item, has catfits. He telephones *Town Trumpet* and says for godsake don't run that item and the editor answers news is news and freedom of the press is the sacred right of every newspaperman. So then while Joe Dough is sitting in his office wondering if it wouldn't be better just to jump out of the window than try to explain to his wife that he bought the fur coat for Julie, the secretary, because she was really cold, what happens but an advertising salesman from *Town Trumpet* is announced. He explains that advertising, after all, is what pays the printer's bill and the editor knows that and is always willing to play ball with an advertiser and they've got so much news anyway that they've got to crowd out some of it and it might as well be the piece about Joe Dough. So Joe buys twelve pages of advertising at a nice rate."

Johnny Fletcher nodded thoughtfully. "About as subtle as a buzz saw. But it just goes to show how dumb people are. Now, me, I'd know right away that if a ginzo was advertising in this rag he's got something to hide."

"That's right," agreed Mort Murray. "but the advertising salesman reminds the advertiser that if he forgets to send in the advertising copy he's got to pay for the space anyway. I used to see issues of *Town Trumpet* without a single ad in them."

"And the editor's name was Egbert Craddock?"

"Yes. He claimed to be the owner of the rag, but the grapevine said it was none other than Matt Boyce. There was talk that he paid Craddock to take the rap."

"A three-year rap? Well, I don't feel so badly now about seeing Boyce's redheaded wife two-timing him. I think I'll go give Matt the ha-ha."

"Give him a snicker for me, too. On account of I'm jealous of a crook like him hitting the jackpot."

8

THEY left Mort Murray's place and walked to Seventh Avenue, where Sam turned automatically in the direction of the subway station at Fourteenth Street. But Johnny held up his hand and whistled to a cab driver.

"Taxis again?" Sam said, sarcastically. "And next week we'll probably be hitchhiking."

"Stick with me and you may be riding in a limousine."

"Yeh! A police limousine."

Ten minutes later Johnny paid off the taxi across from the Grand Central Terminal. They entered a towering office building and as they approached the elevators Johnny suddenly nudged Sam.

"Oh-oh, look who's here!"

"Who . . . where?"

Johnny sidestepped deliberately and collided with a tall man who had an Alabama sheriff's mustache and an absurd potbelly. Johnny's elbow went into the stomach, bringing a 'woof' from the man.

"Hey, look where . . . *Johnny Fletcher!*"

The potbellied man seemed to flinch away from Johnny, who chuckled wickedly, "Jefferson Todd, the great detective."

Sam Cragg gasped. "Jeff . . . holy cats! Jeff Todd with a mustache and a bay window!"

"Johnny Fletcher and Sam Cragg," said Jefferson Todd. "I knew something unpleasant was going to happen today. I had a premonition."

"I didn't feel so good myself when I got up," Johnny said. "Your mustache is on crooked . . . "

Jefferson Todd clapped a hand to his mouth and left his stomach unguarded. Johnny slapped it. " . . . and the soft pillow's slipping."

"Cut it out," snarled Todd.

A gleam came into Sam Crag's eyes. "Don't tell me, cripes, don't tell me; Jeff Todd's *disguised*!"

"Bingo!" said Johnny. "You win the beautiful Navajo Indian blanket. What gives, Jefferson?"

"I'm working. What do you think? Hello and goodbye."

The same to you, Jefferson." Johnny turned and scanned the building directory. He started at the A's and moved along until he finished this part of the alphabet, then put his hand on the directory and let it run down to the B's.

Jefferson Todd exclaimed. "Don't tell me you're going up to see Boy . . . "

"Boyce!" said Johnny. "Hey, *you're* not working working for him."

"No, of course not."

Johnny clucked his tongue against the roof of his mouth. "No, of course not. He wouldn't be hiring *me* if you were already on the job."

"What?" cried Todd. "*You're* working

120

for Matt Boyce?"

Johnny closed his left eye in a deliberate wink. "Just a little detective work, you know. Matt said he'd tried a dopey shamus who bungled the job and — "

"Fletcher!" choked Jefferson Todd.

"Huh?"

"Boyce didn't say that. And you're not working for him."

"Who says we ain't?" bristled Sam Cragg. "You long-legged beanpole."

But Johnny looked up at Jefferson Todd with innocent eyes. "You *are* working for Boyce?"

"Of course I am! Why do you think I'm standing here?"

"How was I to guess? There are forty floors in this building and there should be thousands of tenants . . . "

"I know. But look, Johnny, we're old friends. Let's talk this over . . . "

"Mmm, later. Now, now, Jefferson. I'm late for the appointment . . . "

Todd shot out a bony hand and clutched Johnny's arm. "We can make a good thing out of this — "

"Later," said Johnny. "Sorry, old man . . . " he removed Todd's hand forcibly from his arm and scooted for an open elevator. Todd tried to follow, but Sam Cragg brushed against him and knocked him off balance. Before Todd could recover, Sam had darted into the elevator as the door was closing.

"Twenty-seven," said Johnny.

On the twenty-seventh floor they found a ground-glass door on which was the legend:

2700 – 2710

BOYCE PUBLISHING COMPANY

BLOCKHEAD, THE STRONG MAN

Matt Boyce, *President*

They entered and found themselves in an anteroom some twenty by twenty feet. There was a big director's table in the center, some fine leather-covered chairs and expensive ashstands and pictures of Blockhead The Strong Man all over the walls. Sam regarded them distastefully as Johnny went to a tiny window and rapped on it for attention.

Behind the window, a girl at the switchboard reached up and pushed back the glass a few inches.

"Like to see Matt," Johnny said.

"Who . . . ? Mr. Boyce? Have you an appointment?"

"Tell him it's Johnny — Johnny Fletcher."

The girl lifted the receiver and said into her mouthpiece, "A Mr. Johnny Fletcher to see Mr. Boyce . . . Very well, I'll tell him." She looked up severely at Johnny. "Sorry, but Mr. Boyce says he can't see you."

"Ha-a," said Johnny. "Great guy, Matt. Always kidding. I'll go right in . . . " he reached for the oaken door to his right . . . and couldn't turned the knob. "It's locked!"

"That's right," said the switchboard

operator, closing the glass window.

Johnny took a coin from his pocket and rapped viciously on the glass. The switchboard operator made faces at him, but pushed back the glass again. "Can't you take a hint?"

"No!" cried Johnny. "You tell Matt Boyce that I want to see him right now . . . tell him I want to talk to him about, uh, *Town Trumpet* . . . "

"I'm sorry . . . "

"*Town Trumpet*," snapped Johnny. "Just tell him that and it'll bring him to heel. Go ahead and tell him that, if you know what's good for you."

The girl frowned and hesitated, but then she made the connection. "This Mr. Fletcher insists on speaking to Mr. Boyce. He won't go away. He says it's about . . . *Town Trumpet* . . . Yes?" Se blinked and looked up at Johnny.

"He says he'll see you." She touched a button on the switchboard and the door at Johnny's elbow made a buzzing sound. The knob turned at his touch.

The switchboard operator called,

"Last door on the right."

Johnny and Sam went down a long corridor. They passed an open door and had a quick glimpse of a large room in which a number of artists were huddled over drawing boards. Then they reached Matt Boyce's office and discovered that there was anteroom some ten by ten feet, in which sat Boyce's private secretary, who had undoubtedly been selected by Boyce's wife.

"Mr. Fletcher?"

"And Sam Cragg!"

"You may go in."

Johnny had already opened the inner door, revealing a room that looked like the reading room of the union League Club; at least it was as large and had as many leather armchairs. But it was improved with a couple of couches and a very excellent five-foot bar.

Matt Boyce sat on a throne behind an immense teak-wood desk. His lips were pressed together and his eyes were cold. "What's this *Town Trumpet* stuff?" he asked harshly.

"*Town Trumpet?*" Johnny asked innocently.

"You told the girl you wanted to talk to me about the *Town Trumpet* . . . "

"*Town Trumpet?* Oh — I said something to the girl about your having asked me to come down and I jumped at the opportunity. She misunderstood me. Get it? 'Down and jump at,' What's *Town Trumpet?*"

Matt Boyce started to get up, then dropped back to his chair. "What do you want?"

"Why, I don't know. You asked me to come down today and see you. Remember . . . last night?"

"That was before that policeman came I don't think I have anything to say to you now."

"No? but what would you have said if Egbert Craddock hadn't been killed . . . "

"Craddock!" cried Boyce. "What do you know about Craddock?"

"Oh, wasn't that Soderstrom's real name?"

Boyce looked steadily at Johnny for a moment, before speaking. "Lieutenant Madigan didn't mention Craddock's name."

"Because he's foxy. But he knows because he identified Soderstrom by his fingerprints and they'd be filed as Craddock's."

Matt Boyce picked up an envelope opener and toyed with it. Johnny seated himself in a big armchair and made a pup tent with his hands.

Boyce finally nodded. "Look, you said something to Madigan last night about helping him on a case? He halfway admitted it, but — well, have you ever been a detective?"

"Just an amateur. But I don't mind admitting that I've solved some rather sensational cases that baffled the police no end."

Boyce sniffed. "Modesty isn't one of your vices."

"Why should it be? If I don't tell people how good I am, how are they going to know it. *You* tell people how good *Blockhead* is, don't you?"

"There's a slight difference, but let it pass. How would you like to do some investigating for me?"

"Well," said Johnny. "I'd like to very much, but naturally I'd have to take time off from my regular business and as you know, I do pretty well at it."

"How well?"

"I took in one hundred twenty-eight dollars last night in just a few minutes."

Boyce grunted. "That was an exception. You can't be doing so awfully well, or you wouldn't be living at the 45th Street Hotel."

"Ken Ballinger lives there."

"Yes, that's why I said that. I know what I pay Ballinger."

Johnny cleared his throat. "As it happens the manager of the hotel is an old friend of mine. He'd feel terribly hurt if I stayed anywhere but at his hotel while in New York. So you see . . . "

"I'll give you twenty-five dollars a day."

"*Mister* Boyce! I'm sorry," said Johnny. "As I told you I'm not a regular private detective. Now, I don't know but what you could get some detective for twenty-five to fifty dollars a day. Some lunkhead, uh, Bill Carnegan or Jefferson Todd, but — "

"Jefferson Todd? You know him?"

"From way back! I understand he once caught a kid who robbed apples from a pushcart."

"And you don't think he's a very good investigator?"

"Oh, he's as good as the average that you can get for twenty-five dollars a day. No better, no worse. Why . . . ?"

"Just curious. How much do you think your time is worth?"

"That depends on the kind of case. You want me to find who murdered Egbert Craddock?"

"No."

Johnny blinked. "No? What then . . . ?"

"I'll tell you after you decide to

accept my offer. I'll give you fifty dollars a day."

"For each of us? Well . . . "

"I meant for one. I don't know anything about Block —

"I mean, Cragg, isn't it?"

Sam glowered. "Samuel C. Cragg."

"Very well. Seventy-five dollars a day for the two of you."

"A hundred."

"Seventy-five."

"Seventy-five it is — and five hundred bonus when we wash up the job."

Boyce hesitated, then nodded. "It's a deal, with a three-day time limit."

"Three days is plenty. Now, the retainer . . . "

Boyce pulled open a drawer of his desk and took out a packet of bills. He skimmed off two, then dug into his pocket and brought out a twenty and a five.

He pushed the money across the desk. "There it is, three days' pay. The bonus I'll pay when you deliver."

Johnny waved his hand over the money and it wound up in his palm. "Swell, now what is this little matter you wanted me to investigate?"

"Evidence to divorce my wife."

Johnny exclaimed in chagrin. "I never handled any divorce stuff."

Boyce looked at him coldly. "I agreed to your price, didn't I? You accepted my money — and it's up to you to do whatever I ask. All right, I want evidence that my wife is — well, has been unfaithful. Dan Murphy."

"Must it be Murphy?"

"Don't crowd me too far, Fletcher. I have reason to believe that my wife is in love with Dan Murphy. I want proof that I can use in court."

Sam Cragg was breathing heavily and Johnny shot a quick look at him. The big fellow was scowling fiercely. Johnny sighed. "You can start figuring out your alimony, Mr. Boyce."

"Very well, you have three days. I expect results."

"You'll get them. Mmm, you're

not interested in Egbert Craddock's death?"

"I don't know anyone named Craddock. Hal Soderstrom was murdered, but the police are looking into that. I'm hiring you for something else. Understand?"

Johnny didn't reply. He went to the door, turned and saluted, then went through. As they left the office of Boyce's secretary, Johnny collided with Jim Wilder, whom they had met at the party the night before.

"Say! I was hoping you'd show up," Wilder exclaimed. He began sizing up Sam Cragg and nodded in appraisal. "Look, come in here . . . "

He popped into the room where the artists were huddled over their drawing boards. Fellows," he cried. "This is the man I was telling you about. Blockhead in person!"

Sam Cragg's face was already dark with anger. He retreated to the door. "Go to hell!"

"Show the men your muscles, Sam," Johnny said.

"Yeah, go ahead. I think our drawings have been too stiff, awkward in the delineation of anatomy. I wanted the boys to draw you from life . . . in a lot of different action poses."

"A very good idea," said Johnny Fletcher. "Be worth a lot of money to you, wouldn't it?"

"Naturally, we'd expect to pay for the modeling. I'll talk to Harry Hale about it . . . "

"I heard you," said Harry Hale, coming into the artists' room through a side door.

"Well, what do you think?" Some of the stunts Blockhead does are about as true to life as a bowl of wax fruit. Here . . . !" Wilder snatched up a sheet of bristol board. "Look at this, Blockhead being knocked over by a cannon ball. He looks like a sawdust doll. What we want is reality."

"Okay," said Harry Hale, grinning. "Give him the leopard skin and let him start. Five dollars an hour."

Sam Cragg ducked out of the room.

Johnny turned to Harry Hale. "Oh, come now, you're kidding. Five dollars an hour! A Powers model makes more than that and there are a flock of them. You know yourself Sam is the strongest man in the world. You saw his performance last night . . . "

"That's why I'm offering you five dollars an hour. Because I'm hoping you'll refuse it."

"Nix, Harry!" cried Jim Wilder. "You know Ken's on a bat again and — "

"He's been on bats before and he's always made the deadline."

Yeah, sure, but — "

"Take it up with Boyce," Hale snapped.

Johnny made a quick gesture toward the artists. "If Ken does all the drawing what do these boys do?"

"Fill in the background. Coloring. Ken Ballinger's the animator."

"Like Donald Duck?"

Harry Hale grinned sourly. "In the old days Ken drew the whole book. He did a bangup job, too. But naturally, he couldn't keep up the pace of turning out sixty-four pages every month. We write the story in the next room, break it down to the proper number of frames — six to a page. Then Ken makes rough sketches of the action, featuring Blockhead and the other characters. One of the boys here inks in the action. The others draw in the backgrounds — all of which is planned first. Another does the coloring, puts in the balloons. One of them letters the dialogue in the balloons. It's all well organized. *Blockhead* will never miss a deadline, even if Ken goes on an occasional binge. We can work around him and in a pinch we could even draw the action, although there isn't anyone does it as well as Ken Ballinger."

"I agree with you there, pal," said Johnny. "Ken certainly does a neat job. I imagine he knocks down some real dough."

"He brings a wagon here every payday, so he can take it home with him," Hales said sarcastically. "Well, we've got work to do here. Drop in again sometime, Fletcher."

"I'll do that little thing. Sometime when I can't stay so long."

9

IN the corridor, Sam Cragg muttered. "I don't like that guy Hale."

"I don't exactly like him like a brother, Sammy. But you got to take people as they come." Johnny opened the door leading to the waiting room and recoiled.

"Fletcher," said Jefferson Todd. "I've got to talk to you."

"Certainly, Jeff, give me a ring some day and we'll get together." He brushed past Todd and reached the outer hall, but there Jeff caught up with him. Even Sam's apparently innocent collision with Todd, which almost knocked the long, lean detective off his feet, did not discourage him.

"I want to know why Boyce hired you, Fletcher. No use us working at cross-purposes, is there?"

"Not at all. But you work one way and I work another. You might not see anything in my clues."

"What are they?" Todd asked, eagerly.

Johnny shrugged. "Well, I can tell you, you're wasting your time here, watching the buildings. He won't come."

"But he said he would!"

"People say a lot of things they don't mean. I ask you, *why* would he come?"

"How's he going to reach Boyce if he doesn't?"

"Oh," said Johnny. "But who takes over when Boyce goes home?"

"He's got a bodyguard."

"Mm," said Johnny. "Is the picture Boyce gave you a good one?"

Todd started to reach for his inside breast pocket, then caught himself. "Didn't he give you one?"

"Yes, but I forgot mine at the hotel. Let's see if it's the same."

Todd brought a somewhat faded snapshot from his pocket. It showed three men, wearing fishermen's costumes, hip boots and all. The man in the center was Boyce, Boyce of ten years ago. The man on Boyce's left was a big, muscular man whose face was familiar to Johnny. He had seen it before — in his trunk at the 45th Street Hotel. It was Hal Soderstrom, or Egbert Craddock as he had been known in the old days.

The third man was Dan Murphy.

Johnny handed the snapshot to Sam. "Same snap, isn't it?"

"Huh? Oh sure. Yeah."

"You've seen him, Johnny?" Jeff Todd asked, hopefully.

Johnny screwed up his mouth and nodded slowly.

"Where?" Todd cried. "When?"

"I'll tell you later, Jefferson."

"Why later? Now's as good a time as any. Time is of the essence, man!"

"Of course, that's why we'll make quicker time if I check into this angle before spilling it to you. Where are you staying?"

"The Bagley. Where are you?"

"The 45th Street, as usual. Run over about five this afternoon."

"All right, but I think you could tell me now . . . "

"No. At five o'clock. Down!" he headed for an elevator that had stopped at the floor. He and Sam made it, but Todd stayed behind.

When they reached the lobby of the building Sam said, "You bamboozled Jeff Todd. Wonder why he's waiting for Murphy here? He can't expect to get divorce evidence in such a public place."

"He's doing it the hard way," said Johnny. "I think we'll take a short cut on this job, without the keyholes."

"Yeah?"

"Lulu likes big, strong men. I'll get you and her together, snap your picture — and the dough's ours. Whaddya say?"

A gleam came into Sam's eyes. "Could do. She's nice."

"Huh? You're serious?"

"Why not? You know I like them, uh, you know . . . "

"Yeah," said Johnny thoughtfully. "We'll give Lulu a jingle or something — this afternoon. Couple of people I want to see at the hotel."

"Jill Thayer?"

"And the lad who holes up in Room 717."

"Ken Ballinger?"

"No, he lives upstairs somewhere."

"That's the guy you asked Eddie Miller about. The one with the Swedish name."

"All Johnsons aren't Swedes. I didn't get to tell you about this chappie. Last night when I peeked into Jill's room he came in — with a key."

"Where'd he get it?"

"That's what I want to ask him."

By this time they were well into the Grand Central and descending to the subway, they got into a shuttle train and rode across into Forty-fifth Street. As they approached Dinky Maguire's, Johnny wheeled and headed for the door. Sam started to protest, but Johnny ignored him and entered the narrow cafe.

It was the slack time of the day so there were only a few customers at the bar. They were gathered around Ken Ballinger, the cartoonist, who was complaining drunkenly about the international situation.

"Hi, Ken!" Johnny said cheerfully. "How about a drink?"

Ken blinked owlishly at Johnny Fletcher. "Who're you? I don't know you." Then he shifted to Sam Cragg. "Blockhead, huh? The guy who thinks he's tough. Well, look, I been thinkin' things over and I don't think you're so tough. In fact, I figure on choppin' you down to my size. C'mon, put up your dukes!"

"Gee!" exclaimed Sam. "Whattaman!"

"Hey!" cried the bartender. "No roughstuff in here. I remember you guys from yesterday."

"No roughstuff today," said Johnny. "Look, Ballinger, we're working for

Boyce now. That makes us stablemates, huh?"

"Boyce sent you to find me?"

"Practically. Harry Hale actually suggested it. He's worried about you."

"Yah! All Harry Hale's worried about is himself, the chiseling so-and-so."

"And Jill's worried about you."

An expression of pain crossed Ballinger's face. "Did she send you?"

Johnny looked steadily at Ballinger, then nodded. At that moment the bartender whacked a baseball bat on the bar. "Now, lookee here, you two, you started a roughhouse here yesterday and I won't have another. Get the hell out of here."

Ken Ballinger whirled. "Who you talkin' to, you lousy . . . "

Sam Cragg picked him up under the armpits and carried him to the door. He deposited him on the sidewalk, but kept hold of his arms and continued to propell him forward. Ken was swearing luridly, but Sam silenced him with a kick in the seat of the trousers. Johnny strolled leisurely behind Sam and Ken, but closed up when they entered the 45th Street Hotel. In the elevator he said:

"Seven!"

"Twelve!" Ballinger cried.

"Seven," Johnny repeated firmly and they were let off at the seventh floor. Johnny rapped on the door of Room 721.

It was opened by Jill Thayer. Her face showed annoyance. "You've got the wrong place. This isn't the Times Square Subway Station."

"We brought him here to keep him out of trouble," Johnny said.

"I can take care of myself," Ballinger muttered sullenly.

"Your bosses don't think so," Johnny said, cheerfully. "They're about ready to hire someone else to do Blockhead."

"Let them try. I've got Matt Boyce over a barrel and he damn well knows it — "

"Ken!" Jill Thayer said sharply.

144

"You're talking too much. Why don't you go upstairs and sleep it off?"

"I'm all right. I've only had a few drinks and I'm sick and tired of Matt Boyce thinking he can shove me around. I got a good notion to tell him off. I know where the body's buried."

"In a trunk?"

Jill Thayer turned blazing eyes on him. "You think you're awfully smart, Johnny Fletcher. I've a good notion to tell you what I think of you and your tricks. Why don't you mind you own business?"

"This *is* my business. Someone dumped a corpse in my lap. But it was yours orginally. Remember?"

"That's a lie!"

"I couldda snitched to the cop when he had the heat on me. I didn't. You ought to give me some credit for that."

"I give you credit for being the biggest liar I've ever known."

Johnny assumed an injured air. "And

I was trying to do your boy friend a favor. It isn't just Matt Boyce who's down on him; it's Dan Murphy — "

"Murphy!" cried Ballinger. "Why that lousy strip-tease impresario, I'll boot him up and down Forty-second Street. What I don't know about that — "

"Ken!" Jill Thayer stepped forward and slapped his face. Ken took the blow and looked at her stupidly for a moment. Then he began to cry. It was a gradual process. First his mouth and chin quivered, then tears began to stream down his cheeks, and finally his body shook from wracking sobs.

"Get out of here," Jill Thayer shouted at Johnny Fletcher.

Sam had already backed out. Johnny shrugged and stepped to the elevator. He pushed the down button.

"Up," Sam Cragg said.

The red light showed over the door. Johnny pushed Sam into the elevator.

When they reached the lobby Johnny

steered Sam to the door. The latter growled, "What was the idea of that business, Johnny?"

"Talk. Get somebody mad and they spill things. Ken Ballinger says he knows where the bodies are buried. He's got something on both Boyce and Murphy."

"He talked like blackmail," Sam said. "Me, I don't care a lot for blackmailers."

"I don't either. But remember what Mort Murray said about Matt Boyce owning *Town Trumpet*. If that's true, he deserves to be blackmailed himself."

"Just the same I don't like it. I can't say that I like Boyce, but we did take his dough — "

"That's right. We're working for *him* and that's where we're going now. To look up Dan Murphy. He's in the girlie movie business it seems. Ballinger said strip-tease impresario and he said something about kicking him up Forty-second Street, so that's where we ought to find him.

"Yeah, but there are a dozen movie houses between Seventh and Eighth Avenue alone."

"Not that many. It just looks like it. I'll find out in a minute."

10

THEY had turned into Broadway and were approaching Forty-second Street. Johnny stopped at a newsstand. "Hi, Mac," he greeted the newsie. "Look, I'm going over to see Dan Murphy and I forgot which theater he hangs out at."

"The hot one," replied the newsie. "The Pom Pom."

"Thanks, pal."

They turned west on Forty-second Street, passed two cheap movie houses and reached the Pom Pom.

Johnny breezed past the ticket window and moved upon the ticket taker. "I'm going in to see Dan Murphy," he said."

"Sure," replied the ticket-taker. "After you buy a ticket."

"Nix, I'm not going in to see the show — "

"Ha-ha-ha," the ticket-taker laughed mirthlessly.

"Then tell Dan Murphy to come here."

"Can't leave the door. Buy a ticket or scram."

Johnny muttered under his breath and went back to the ticket window where he paid for two tickets. He thrust them at the ticket taker.

"All right, now where's Dan Murphy's office?"

"Right inside on the left. But he ain't here. He hadda go out."

"When's he coming back?"

"Can't say. I only work here. Maybe a minute, maybe an hour."

"We can wait, Johnny, can't we?" Sam asked.

Johnny caught the eagerness in Sam's tone and shook his head. "All right, Sammy."

They went into the theater. A film so old and faded that it was streaked was being shown on the screen. Johnny and Sam found seats on the aisle near the rear.

The picture ran for twenty minutes, then the house lights went on. "I'll see if Dan's come in," Johnny said. He got up and went to Murphy's office. The door was locked.

He returned to his seat beside Sam, and they watched the beginning of the old girlie film.

Johnny left his seat once more. This time he found Dan Murphy's office open. Murphy was sitting behind a desk wearing a derby and chewing an unlighted cigar.

"Hi, Murphy," Johnny greeted him.

Murphy scowled, then recognized Johnny. "The book salesman. Say, I was just thinking about you. That wasn't a bad routine you and your stooge worked. He looked pretty good in the leopard skin, too."

"Just like Blockhead. By the way didn't you have something to do with Blockhead once?"

Murphy grimaced. "I invented him."

"You did? I thought it was Matt Boyce's idea?"

"Yah!" jeered Murphy. "All Boyce ever invented was ways to muscle in on somebody else's ideas. I discovered Blockhead and started him on the way to his first million circulation. Then Boyce stepped in and took him away from me."

"How could he do that if the book was doing so well?"

"That's what made me so sore. I was publishing comics for four-five years on a shoestring. I just about starved, but the printer carried me. They can do that, you know. Even if they only get two-thirds of their money it's worthwhile for them to keep a job going. Takes up the slack in the shop. Anyway, I was on the books for a measly fifty grand. Six months of Blockhead and I'd have wiped it out. But no, Boyce gets wind of a good thing and what does he do? He buys into the printer and puts the squeeze on me. Kicks me out and takes over Blockhead. In six months he owned the print shop. It was that crook Harry

Hale who sold me out. I picked up Hale when he was wearing turtle-neck sweaters because he couldn't afford to have his shirts laundered."

"Hale used to work for you? Ballinger, too, I suppose?"

"Yeah, sure. The kid had a good idea but didn't know what to do with it. I put it over for him."

"Blockhead was really Ballinger's idea?"

"Oh yeah, but ideas are a dime a dozen. Ballinger peddled Blockhead all around. Even the newspaper syndicates turned him down. It was pretty amateurish. I pumped it up and got him to do snappier drawings then sold the strip. Another publisher might have muffed it."

"So now you're managing a girlie joint."

Murphy looked sharply at Johnny. "Eh?"

"I mean, isn't it funny the way us smart guys always lose out and the dummies clean up?"

"That's *very* funny. Only I didn't say Matt Boyce was a dummy. He's anything but. That guy's smarter than you and I put together. And crookeder."

Johnny smacked his lips. "In business. But you're getting even. You know — last night."

"What about it?"

"Why, I like redheads myself."

Murphy's eyes narrowed. "You're wrong about Lulu. She's divorcing Boyce."

"Really? But doesn't she have to, well, leave her husband's home to do that?"

"She has," Murphy said, savagely. "Now, what else can I tell you that Boyce ought to know?"

"Boyce, ah?"

"You're a dick, ain't you? That phony song-and-dance last night didn't fool me a damn bit. And why're you here today?"

"My pal wanted to see a good leg show."

"The show's out there."

"Okay, Murph, I can take a hint."

Johnny crossed the foyer and entered the auditorium, where bedlam reigned. He found Sam Cragg clapping and whistling. He had to tap him twice before Sam turned.

"Come on, Sam," Johnny said, sharply. "You've see enough."

"Enough? Heck, the show hardly started."

"For you it's ended. We're going to the public library to do some refined reading — to wipe this out of your mind."

Sam got up and walked out to the foyer with Johnny, but he was quite unhappy about it. "What can you see at the public library?"

"We're working men. We can't take any money at a leg show."

They left the theater and crossing the street caught a crosstown bus in which they rode to Fifth Avenue, where they got off and entered the big New York Library.

Inside Johnny made inquiry at the information desk and was directed to the periodical room. In the latter room the attendant looked at him in surprise. "*Town Trumpet*? The files are out at the moment."

"Out? I thought you didn't let people take them from the room."

"We don't, but you see — "

"Johnny Fletcher!" called Lieutenant Madigan.

Johnny whirled. Lieutenant Madigan was sitting at a desk a short distance away. A number of bound volumes were at his elbow and one of them was open before him.

Johnny went over. "*Town Trumpet*?" he read the title on the volume. "Hot stuff, isn't it?"

"Uh-huh, and I suppose you were going to read the back issues of *Little Ladies*?"

An attendant came up. "Quiet, please; this is a reading room."

Johnny snickered. "And this is a cop; you can't tell him to keep quiet."

Lieutenant Madigan glared at the library attendant. Then he grunted at Johnny. "So you're sticking your nose into it?"

"Some people collect stamps. What'd Craddock go up for?"

"Craddock?"

"Oh, I'm not *that* far behind you, Lieutenant. Craddock was Soderstrom. He was editor of *Town Trumpet*. But who'd he shake down? I mean, the one that proved it on him."

A woman named Smithson. Craddock got a tough break. He started this squeeze, but before he could wind it up the lady's husband caught her anyway, so it didn't make any difference and she turned the heat on Craddock. But she doesn't figure in this. She married a cowboy six years ago."

"And Smithson?"

"He lost his money after that and jumped out of a window. So *he* couldn't have done it to Craddock."

"Then who did?"

"That's why I'm reading. But I'm

about ready to quit. The last issue of *Town Trumpet* came out almost seven years ago. A lot of people mentioned in it are still around, but the trouble is there are so many of them it'd take months to check on all of them. And that might not have been the motive at all."

"I think you've got something there, Maddy. If Craddock went up the river seven years ago, it's four since he came back. Why wait four years?"

Madigan frowned. "That's what I was thinking. but I didn't want to pass up any bets. Look, what's your angle?"

"Boyce could tell a lot of things."

"Yeah, if we still used rubber hoses But we don't — and we never did use them on guys worth a million bucks. Boyce is a pretty cool customer."

"He's got a wife. She's divorcing Boyce."

Madigan's eyes lit up. "Since when?"

"Since today, I gather."

"Then she's still plenty sore. Mmm, she may talk."

"Women do talk," Johnny said. He'd met Lulu Boyce only fleetingly, but he had sized her up instantly. Madigan would get from her exactly what Lulu wanted to tell him. Nothing more. But Madigan would be occupied for a while. At the moment he was one step ahead of Johnny; Johnny had to pass him.

Madigan gathered up the books and took them back to the desk. He walked with Johnny and Sam to the outside door of the library. "Which way are you going, fellows?"

"Back to our hotel, I guess," Johnny said. "It looks like it's going to rain and we got a couple of raincoats or something there."

He did go back to the hotel with Sam, but they remained in their room only long enough to pick up their rather ancient raincoats. With the coat over his arm Johnny hesitated.

Finally he nodded. "Put on your raincoat, Sam, and turn down the brim of your hat. And scowl, Fine!

159

Now, you look just like a flatfoot. Keep your mouth shut and whenever I look at you, grunt."

"Who you going to razzle-dazzle?"

"Mr. Tommy Johnson, down on the seventh floor. I'm awfully curious about him. Why he's got the key to Jill Thayer's room, when her boy friend is supposed to be Ken Ballinger."

"Gosh, I wouldn't have thought it of her."

"Neither would I. So . . . scowl!"

11

THEY descended to the seventh floor and moved upon Room 717. Johnny beat a tattoo upon the door. There was no response and he gave the door another massage.

It was opened a few inches by Tom Johnson. Sam Cragg shoved both the door and Tom Johnson and they crowded into the room. Johnson's sullen face showed alarm.

"Hey, what's the idea?"

"Your name Tom Johnson?" Johnny asked curtly.

"Yes, but who're you . . . ?"

Johnny looked at Sam and the latter scowled fiercely. Johnny said, "Where're you from and how long've you lived at this hotel?"

"I've been here about three weeks. My home's in Iowa."

"Why'd you come to New York?"

"Why does anybody come? To get a job."

"Aren't there any jobs in Iowa?"

Johnson made an impatient gesture. "Not my kind. I'm an artist. Cartoonist."

Johnny looked around the room. "Where's your drawing board?"

"Haven't got one with me. I'm trying to get a job with a magazine. But look, you're the fellow who was in Jill's room last night. I don't believe you're a — "

"What were *you* doing in her room?" Johnny snapped.

"Nothing. Jill's a friend of mine. I told her about you and she said you weren't a policeman."

Johnny looked at Sam and the latter produced a ferocious scowl and a loud grunt. "Miss Thayer said that? Do you know the jam she's in herself?"

"She isn't in any jam," Johnson replied, with heat. "And I don't see what right you have asking me questions."

"A man was murdered in this

162

hotel yesterday. We're asking everybody questions."

"By what right? Jill said you weren't a policeman."

"No. And what do you think he (pointing at Sam) is?"

The door behind Johnny was slammed violently open and Jill Thayer, her eyes blazing, came into the room. "He's a thickheaded stumblebum, that's what he is. And you, Johnny Fletcher, you're an insolent, snooping, busybody. I'm telling you for the last time to keep out of my affairs."

Tom Johnson took a quick step forward, cocking his right fist. "So you're not a cop, eh? Well, then . . . " he let fly with the fist, Johnny tried to duck and bumped into Jill Thayer. The fist caught him high on the forehead.

He grunted and, lowering his head, stepped in. But he was too late. Sam Cragg had caught up young Tom Johnson and thrown him six feet on to the bed. Then he brushed his hands.

"Okay, Johnny."

Johnny looked at Jill Thayer. Her face was cold. He shrugged and stepped past her. He walked to the elevator, Sam following. As they stood waiting, Johnny shot a quick glance at the door of Room 721. The door was closed.

He inhaled deeply and stepping forward, tried the doorknob. The door opened. He stuck in his head and pulled it out quickly.

"What's the idea?" Sam asked.

"Just wanted to see if she got rid of Ballinger. She did."

The elevator door opened and they stepped in. As they reached the lobby, Johnny took a pamphlet from his raincoat pocket. It was a sixteen-page booklet with the title *National Bookhunter*.

"Where'd you get that?" Sam exclaimed.

"Oh, just picked it up." They reached the door and Johnny looked out into a heavy drizzle. He pressed the booklet together, then let it fall open. It had been creased back between

164

pages six and seven.

He looked at the pages. There was a heading at the top of each: 'Books wanted' and the text consisted of dealers' listings. There were four groups of listings on page six, two on seven.

All but six of the listings were from dealers out of New York City. The address of the first New York City was down in Greenwich Village. But the other was on West Fortieth Street. The listing read:

Hockmeyer's Books, West Fortieth Street . . .
New York City
Brower. *Self Help in Piano Study*
Bosworth. *Geology of Mid-Continent Oil Field*
Birth, J. H. *Safety Match*
Lyman. *Ralston's Ring*
Shellrock Iowa *H-Way*, June 1952 (A school paper)

"What is it?" Sam Cragg asked.
"A trade journal; for rare book

dealers, I guess. Come on, the rain won't hurt us."

Johnny stepped out into the drizzle. They walked to Broadway and turned south. At Times Square they crossed to Seventh and continued on it to Fortieth, where they turned right. A hundred feet from the corner they came to a long, narrow book shop. "This is it," said Johnny.

They went into the store. In front was a table on which several hundred books were being offered at three for a dollar. Shelves lined both sides of the room, but very few of the books on them were new.

There were no customers in the place. Halfway down the room an incredibly fat man sat behind a desk reading a volume of Swinburne's poems.

Johnny said, "Mr. Hockmeyer?"

"Yes," wheezed the fat man, "but just look around. If you see anything you like, ask the price."

"Swell, but you may not have what I'm looking for."

"What is it?"

"A high school paper printed about ten years ago."

Hockmeyer lowered his volume of poetry and looked from Johnny Fletcher to Sam Cragg. "I see. Would it be the Shellrock, Iowa, high school paper?"

"That's right."

"Well, what about it?"

"That's what I was going to ask you. According to this copy of the *National Bookhunter*, you've been advertising for that school paper?"

"That's right. I ran the ad four times."

"And did it bring results?"

"Yes."

"You got a copy of the paper."

"Yes."

Johnny cleared his throat. "Who ordered it? What was the name of the person?"

The fat bookdealer cleared his throat. "I run a legitimate business here. If people want rare and out-of-print books and publications I try to get them for

167

them. I don't ask for their pedigree. The man who asked me to get him that paper gave the name of Egbert Craddock and that's all I know about him."

"But you can describe him, can't you?"

"I'm not very good at that sort of thing. Not observant of people. He was about medium height I'd say, medium weight. Maybe forty or forty-five."

"But he gave you an address, didn't he?"

"The Burco Building."

"Not bad," said Johnny. "For a man who isn't observant you certainly remember a lot of things about a minor business transaction."

"Oh, I have special occasion to remember this. I looked it all up just an hour ago."

"Eh? How come?"

"The other detective . . . the tall thin one with the walrus mustache — "

"Jefferson Todd!" cried Sam Cragg.

"I'll be damned," Johnny swore.

168

"You told him everything?"

"Just what I've told you. He had a picture of this Craddock, who I understand was murdered yesterday. Odd, I only gave him the paper yesterday morning. It was a hard item to get. People don't save their high school papers and in obscure places like that you don't find anyone who reads the book trade journals. Matter of fact I had to buy it through another dealer. Ran the price up pretty high."

"How much?"

"Seventy-five dollars. That's what I had to charge Craddock. Naturally I have to make a profit on a transaction. The Waterloo dealer probably paid twenty-five for it."

"Did you give his name to this skinny dick?"

"Yes. It's Langford. Quite a reliable dealer. Has a good rating." Hockmeyer picked up his Swinburne. "If there's anything else — "

"I guess that about covers the subject."

Johnny sighed and left the store with Sam. It had stopped raining, but the sidewalks were still wet. "Either I'm awfully dumb on this business," Johnny groused to Sam, "or these other birds are getting inside information."

"From whom?"

"Boyce . . . Hale . . . Ballinger; they all knew Craddock. Even Murphy."

"Yeah, but how'd the kid — Johnson — get into this?"

"He comes from Iowa. Maybe he went to the Shellrock High School."

"Then he ought to know about the paper!"

"Maybe yes, maybe no. I think I ought to have another talk with the boy, but I'm afraid he's antisocial by this time."

"I could make him talk."

Johnny shook his head. They had reached Times Square. Johnny looked east up Forty-second, scowling. Then finally he shrugged and turned north to cross the street.

12

AN automobile horn beeped and Johnny made a frantic leap to escape. He reached the sidewalk in two jumps, missed and sprawled headlong on the concrete. He didn't hear the rip, but the cold wet pavement touching his entire right thigh caused him to scramble up.

He howled in chagrin, for his trouser leg was slit from the thigh to below the knee.

"Holy cow!" Sam Cragg cried when he saw the gash.

"There ought to be a law against taxicabs," Johnny said, bitterly. "The so-and-so didn't even stop and now what am I going to do? This suit's absolutely ruined."

"Gee, mister, that's tough," sympathized a passerby.

Johnny shot a quick glance around

and saw that a dozen people had already congregated. "Beat it," he snarled, "whaddya think this is, a free show?"

He turned and stalked across the street, wrapping the raincoat around him. Sam followed. "There's a tailor on Forty-fourth Street," he said.

"He couldn't fix this suit. And look at the mud. I've got to get a new suit — or at least a pair of pants that will match the coat reasonably. It'll have to be secondhand because the coat's pretty well along. I'll . . . " He stopped and stared at the Times Building.

Then suddenly he began to whistle softly. "I wonder if I can get away with it. Mmm, the pants are ruined so I can't lose anything by trying, Yeah — Peabody's been too doggone smug lately, anyway."

A worried look came to Sam's face. "What're you scheming, Johnny? You've got that — cripes, don't do anything to get us in Dutch."

"I need a new suit," Johnny said

doggedly. "And I'm going to get it. Come on!" He led Sam into the Times Building and down to the subway station. Passing through the turnstiles they entered the washroom, where Johnny slipped off his raincoat and removed his trousers. He emptied the pockets, putting the stuff into his coat pockets. Sam watched him anxiously. When Johnny began ripping the ruined pair of trousers below the knees, he cried out in chagrin.

"What're you doing, Johnny?"

Johnny finished ripping off one trouser leg and coolly started on the second. "They're no good the way they were, are they?" With a savage jerk he ripped off the second trouser leg. He punched a hole in the top of each foot-long section of trouser leg. He then tore a handkerchief into narrow strips and tying a couple of sections together fastened one end of the manufactured cord to the trouser leg and the others to his suspenders.

Then he pulled both trouser legs

over his feet and put on the raincoat. Buttoning it tightly he straightened. "How does it look, Sammy?" he asked.

"All right." said Sam, dubiously, "but if your coat happens to flap open . . ."

"I'll see that it doesn't. All right, now come on."

"You're going out on the street that way?"

"Isn't windy, is it?"

"No, but . . . " Sam groaned. "All right, but if the cops grab you I'm not with you."

They left the subway station and climbed up to Times Square. "Now, here's what you do, Sam," Johnny explained as they walked toward Forty-fifth Street. "When we get into the hotel lobby go up to the desk and stay there in full sight. If Eddie Miller's around chew the rag with him. You need an absolutely airtight alibi — "

"What for?" cried Sam, in alarm. "What're you going to pull?"

"You'll see. The less you know about

it, the more surprised you'll be. Just remember, don't get out of sight for a single instant . . . "

They turned into Forty-fifth Street and approached the hotel. As they entered Johnny exclaimed softly. "There's Peabody, stick with him . . . Afternoon, Mr. Peabody, a little damp outside, isn't it?"

Peabody sniffed. "You can expect it to be damp, when it's raining."

"Quite so, quite so. Well, I guess I'll run up and take a hot bath." Leaving Sam with Peabody, Johnny stepped into an elevator.

Sam Cragg cleared his throat. "Look, Mr. Peabody, did I ever tell you about the dog farm I inherited out in Missouri?"

"No," said Mr. Peabody. "But I don't imagine it amounted to so very much . . . "

"Ah, but that's where you're wrong, Mr. Peabody. There was two hundred of the finest St. Bernard dogs you ever saw in your life. And a beautiful forty-acre farm with a swell house on it. Boy, it certainly looked good when I first saw it — "

"Then why didn't you stay out there?"

"Because the dogs ate too much. Imagine! Two hundred pooches and each of them eating five pounds of food a day — a half ton."

"You must tell me about it some time — when I've nothing else to do. If you'll excuse me, now . . . "

"Wait a minute," Sam cried, desperately. "I want to ask you something."

"Yes?"

"Uh, it's something important. Well, not exactly important."

"No."

"Huh? Whaddya mean, no? You don't know yet what I'm going to ask, do you? It's uh, about, well, about . . . "

"Mr. Peabody," called the desk clerk. "Will you take this call please? It's — Mr. Fletcher in Room 821."

Peabody looked coldly at Sam Cragg

and sniffed. "Tell him I'm busy," he said to the clerk.

The latter shook his head. "I think you'd better talk to him, Mr. Peabody. He's quite irate. Says someone's stolen his trousers."

"What?" Peabody blinked, then took a quick step to the desk and scooped up the phone. "What nonsense is this now, Fletcher?" he cried. "What . . . ? That's ridiculous. No! Please . . . I won't stand for that. Don't you dare do that. I'll have you arrested. No, no! I'll come right up!"

Mr. Peabody slammed the receiver on the hook and turned a distorted face to Sam Cragg. "That partner of yours; I'll . . . I'll throw him out of the hotel."

"You and who else?" Sam challenged truculently.

Peabody wheeled and signaled to Eddie Miller. "Eddie, come with me. And you, too, Cragg."

"What's the matter with you?" Sam snapped. "Have you gone nuts?"

"No, but Fletcher . . . ahrr! Eddie, when we get upstairs I want you to stand by the door and see that nothing is taken out — nothing, understand?"

"Yes, Mr. Peabody." Eddie Miller said, meekly. Then catching Sam's eye he winked.

They stepped out of the elevator and moved in a body to the door of Room 821. "All right, Eddie!" Peabody said sharply. He reached out and pounded on the door of the room.

It was jerked open instantly by Johnny Fletcher. Johnny was wearing striped shorts and a shirt. His hair was wet and moisture still glistened on his face.

"What kind of a hotel is this, Peabody?" he cried. "A man steps into the bathroom to take a bath and when he comes out some pants burglar has entered his room and stolen his pants. What've you got here — a den of thieves?"

"Mr. Fletcher," said Peabody, his nostrils flaring, "Please lower your voice. There are other guests in this hotel."

"Robbers!" Johnny roared.

"No one stole your trousers," Peabody said, coldly. "You've mislaid them — and if I find them, you'll be sorry."

"Go ahead and find them!"

"I will!"

Peabody entered the room, took a quick glance into the bathroom and headed straight for the window. He poked out his head and looked down into the courtyard eight floor below. When he pulled in his head he was biting his lips.

He got down on his hands and knees and looked under the bed. Then he tried the big trunk and the single clothes closet. Finally he ripped the bed part and raised the mattress.

By that time he was beginning to perspire. "They must be here, Fletcher," he said angrily. "You've hidden them somewhere."

"Do I look crazy? Why would I hide

them? Hey . . . wait a minute. I had some money — "

"No," screamed Peabody. "Don't start that. The hotel's not responsible for money. There's a sign on the back of every door says you've got to check valuables downstairs . . . "

"Pants, too?" Johnny scooped up his coat and plunged his hand into the side pocket. Then he grunted. "My money's here. Lucky for you. But what about my pants?"

Peabody gritted his teeth and got down on all fours and began patting the rug to make sure there were no lumps in it. He went into the bathroom, came out and began searching the room again. But he couldn't find Johnny's trousers.

And at last he gave up.

"All right, they're not here," he conceded. "I'm sorry, but that's all there's to it."

"What am I going to do?" Johnny cried. "They were the only pair of pants I owned. You think I'm a millionaire that I own two suits? It's your fault that you allow thieves in this hotel and I tell you I'm holding you responsible."

Peabody brushed his hands together. "I'm sorry, but the hotel is *not* responsible."

"The hell it isn't, I'll sue you — "

"For a ten-dollar pair of trousers? Don't be absurd."

"Ten dollar hell. That suit was worth seventy-five dollars and the coat's no good without the pants."

"You can buy a pair that'll match reasonably close . . . "

"How? I haven't got any pants to wear."

"Sam Cragg can go out and get you some."

"Yeah, sure, Johnny," Sam volunteered.

"No," Johnny said. "Sam can't go out and get me a pair of pants. He can't because I won't let him. It's the hotel's fault that my pants were stolen and I won't leave this room until I get a new suit."

Peabody snickered. "You'll get hungry

after a while." He went to the door.

"On second thought," Johnny said, grimly. "I'm going down to the lobby right now — like this."

"You wouldn't dare. I'll have you arrested!"

"Do that," Johnny snapped. "Fetch in the cops. They'll have to take me down to the station like I am — and if you think the newspaper boys won't see a story in that you've got another think coming. It'll look good in the papers — 'Guest's pants robbed by burglar at 45th Street Hotel' — "

Peabody clapped his hand to his forehead. "Oh, what did I ever do to earn this? Why do you come to this hotel, Fletcher? It's such a peaceful place when you're not here."

"There's a draft here with that door open," Johnny said. "I think I'll go down to the lobby."

"Don't you dare!"

Johnny brushed Peabody aside and stepped into the hall. Miller regarded him with tongue in cheek. Johnny

182

pushed the elevator button. "Going down!"

Peabody hurtled out of the room and grabbed Johnny by the arm. "Please, Fletcher, you can't — "

"Do I get a new suit?"

"Well — a new pair of pants."

"No, whole suit or nothing. Going down . . . "

The red light showed overhead and Peabody tugged frantically on Johnny's arm. "All right, all right."

"Sam! You know my size. Don't take too long. I'll wait a half hour and if the suit isn't here by then I'm coming down to the lobby . . . "

The elevator door began to open and Johnny leaped back into his room. It was well that he did, for there were two women in the elevator.

Down in the lobby, Peabody took a card from his pocket and wrote on it. "Take this to Hahn's where I buy my own suits. It's right on the corner. And remember — fifty dollars is the limit."

183

"Fifty?" Sam asked. "You can't get much of a suit for fifty bucks."

"That's all I pay for my own. If it's good enough for me — "

"It ain't good enough for Johnny! Maybe I better go and tell him what you said."

"No! All right, go up to sixty-five. But that's the absolute limit."

"Okay, pal," Sam Cragg said. "but I don't think Johnny'll like it."

He put the card into his pocket and walked to Hahn's big store on Broadway. "I want to get a nifty suit for a pal of mine," Sam told the clerk. "He's five feet ten inches tall and weighs a hun'ert and seventy. He's pretty big in the shoulders for a skinny guy."

"About a thirty-six, I'd say," said the clerk. "Now, here's a nice piece of material."

"Nah, it's too gloomy looking. Haven't you got something with some snap?"

"Snap, eh? Step over here, please. Now, here's a nice British lounge model. perhaps a trifle, ah, too vivid?"

"Whaddya mean vivid? I want something snappy."

The half hour was just about up when Sam Cragg opened the door of Room 821 and found Johnny dressed in shirt and shorts stretched out on one of the twin beds.

"Ah, you got it," Johnny exclaimed, getting up. "I hope you selected something good."

"I bought a pip," Sam replied. "Peabody said I couldn't go over sixty-five, but I hiked it up to seventy bucks and got a swell suit. Look . . . !" He broke the string of the parcel and reaching in produced the coat.

"Ohmigawd!" cried Johnny in horror.

"Like it? I thought you would."

"Take it back," Johnny howled. "I wouldn't wear that to a Harlem cockfight. Jumping Joe Johnson, you could hear that suit eight miles away, it's so loud."

Sam looked injured. "Loud? I think it's kinda snappy. These plaid checks

185

are the very latest, the clerk said. Gosh, I'd like a suit like that myself."

"Take it back; it's hurting my eyes. Get me something I can wear down the street without having everyone look at me."

Sam sighed wearily and put the suit back into the box. He rode down in the elevator and encountered Peabody in the lobby. The latter stared at the suitbox. "What's the matter, is he finicky about the fit?"

"No, I guess it fits all right, but he thought it was maybe a little too loud."

"I didn't think they came too loud for him. Let me see it." Peabody twisted up a corner of the box and peered in. Then he exclaimed and tugged the coat out of the box. He held it up before him and cried out in triumph. "Ha! So he wants to exchange it, does he? Well, I'm stepping right to the telephone the moment you leave and I'm telling Hahn's not to make the exchange. A suit he wanted and he got. I didn't guarantee the color. Let him wear this; it'll teach him a lesson."

"You mean you won't let him exchange the suit?"

"That's exactly what I said."

"But this suit cost seventy bucks. Maybe I can exchange it for one for less money?"

Greed struggled with revenge on Peabody's face, then revenge won. He shook his head. "No, it'll be worth it to see him wear that suit. Take it up to him. I wash my hands of the whole matter. He's got the suit; now let him wear it."

Sam returned to Room 821. "Peabody says it's no dice on the exchange. He won't let the store do it."

A glint came to Johnny's eyes. "Okay," he said. "I didn't think the worm had it in him. All right, I'll wear the horse blanket and I hope Peabody's eyes hurt him every time he looks at me."

He put on the suit and looked at

himself in the mirror, wincing.

"It's a swell fit," said Sam Cragg. "By the way, Johnny, how'd you ever get rid of the pants legs?"

"Tore them in pieces and flushed them down the toilet bowl. I hope the pipes get clogged up somewhere. Well, let's go and see if any dogs bark at me."

As he opened the door, Eddie Miller fell in, landing on his hands and knees. He picked himself up, grinning ruefully.

"I was just about to knock."

"I'll bet you were. Did you ever get a hatpin stuck into your eye, through a keyhole?"

"Women don't wear hatpins any more. I was bringing up this telephone slip. You got a call while you were out. He thrust a slip of paper at Johnny.

Johnny read: "Mr. Boyce telephoned. He wants you to come to his apartment at five o'clock."

"It's four-thirty now," said Eddie Miller. "Thought you'd want to know."

"Thanks, Eddie. Remind me to give you a dime sometime."

Eddie pretended to see Johnny's suit for the first time and held his hand up to his eyes, as if dazzled. "That's quite a suit," he said.

"Isn't it? I like snappy clothes. Well, don't put any Mickey Fins in the ice water, Eddie."

"I just remembered something I seen yesterday, Mr. Fletcher. I don't think you'd be interested in it, but your friend Lieutenant Madigan might be glad if you'd tip him off. I know you're not working on the case yourself — "

Johnny looked sharply at Eddie. "What is it?"

"Oh, I guess it's not really so *very* important. It's about this fella who got bumped yesterday."

"Do I have to choke it out of you?"

Eddie smirked. "Maybe I don't remember it so well, after all."

Johnny scowled at Eddie and took a dollar from his pocket. Eddie looked at the money without much interest. Johnny added another dollar.

Edie said, "It's beginning to come now. If you could refresh my memory a little stronger — "

"I'm curious only two dollars' worth. Madigan wouldn't pay you anything."

Eddie took the money and stowed it away. "I was taking a guest up to the seventh floor and I saw this Soderstrom going into Room 717. Johnson was with him."

"Yes?"

"That's all. They closed the door."

"It was right before I went out for lunch — and I eat at twelve. The papers said he must have been killed about that time."

Johnny nodded thoughtfully, "Did you see Soderstrom at the hotel before yesterday?"

"Oh, sure, he came here once or twice a week. Usually with Ken Ballinger. I didn't know his name, but I knew him by sight."

"Thank you, my boy, thank you.

Keep that information under your hat and I may throw you another bone or two."

Eddie Miller grinned and departed. Johnny and Sam followed immediately, riding down in the elevator with the bellboy. Down in the lobby, they started toward the door just as Jefferson Todd, still wearing his disguise, came in.

Johnny groaned. "What brings you here, Jeff?"

"You asked me to come at five, don't you remember?"

"Yeah sure, but I forgot I have an appointment. Couldn't you make it later?"

"No, I'm hot on something. I just wanted to ask you a question or two about Dan Murphy."

You can find him at the Pom Pom Theater on Forty-second Street."

I know. I was there. He said you'd been there."

"Oh, so I beat you there. I understand you're interested in rare books."

"What? You're working on that

angle? Look, let's talk this over."

"Can't, I told you I've got a date."

"So have I. With Lulu Boyce. But it can wait. This — "

"Sorry," said Johnny, brushing past Jeff. "My date can't wait."

He hurried out of the hotel, Sam blocking interference. At the curb, Johnny signaled to a taxicab. As he and Sam Cragg climbed in, Jefferson Todd attempted to follow. "We can talk in the cab — "

"Can't you take a hint?" Sam growled. "We don't want you, see?"

He put his big hand on Jeff Todd's chest and pushed him back.

As the cab started off, Johnny gave the address of Matt Boyce's East River apartment and fifteen minutes later they were riding up the elevator.

They got off the elevator at the top floor and climbed the flight to the penthouse, where Johnny rang the doorbell.

There was no response and he rang a couple of times more. At last he tried the door. It was open. The moment he stepped inside a premonition of disaster swept over him.

"Easy, Sam," he said, sharply. "Don't touch anything."

"Nobody's at home," said Sam. "Lulu must have fired all the help before she went."

"Probably. Make it tough for Matty to get new help. But why'd he call me if he wasn't going to be here?" They walked through the big room where the party had been held the night before. Johnny hesitated a moment before the bedroom door, then pushed it open.

Matt Boyce was lying on the thick rug. His eyes were glassy; his mouth was open. He was dead.

13

JOHNNY FLETCHER backed violently into Sam Cragg. The latter, pushed off balance, had a quick glimpse of Matt Boyce lying on the floor.

"For gossakes!" he gasped.

Johnny pulled shut the door of the bedroom. "This is no place for us, Sammy boy. Let's scram out of here as quickly as we can."

"What're we waiting for?" cried Sam. He started across the big living room in tremendous strides. Ten feet from the door he skidded to a stop.

"Anybody home?" called a voice.

"Jefferson Todd!" moaned Johnny.

Todd, who had already opened the door, popped into the room. "Oh, here you are, Johnny. I followed you."

"What for?" Johnny rasped.

"Well, I had a date here myself

at five. I tried to tell you and you wouldn't listen."

"Did Matt Boyce ask you to call?"

"He left word at my office. I telephone in every hour and my secretary gave me the message."

"Did she get it from Boyce himself?"

"I don't know. Say, why all the questions?"

Johnny drew a deep breath. "Take a look in the bedroom."

Automatically Jefferson Todd took a couple of steps forward, then he stopped and regarded Johnny through slitted eyes. "What's in the bedroom?"

"Matt Boyce . . . and he isn't sleeping."

"What do you mean . . . ?"

"The business. Go ahead, take a look."

"No, I'll take your word . . . Why'd you do it?"

"Cut it out," Johnny growled. "I didn't bump Matt Boyce."

"I didn't say you did, but I think I'll be running along now."

"No, you won't." Johnny said.

"I think I will."

Sam Cragg wheeled and flanked Jefferson Todd, cutting him off from the door. "Try and get past me, Jeff," he invited. "I've always wanted to poke you one."

Todd's upper lip curled. "The elevator man brought you up before me. He'll remember that."

Johnny sighed. "Okay, I'll be a good citizen." He crossed the room to a telephone and picked it up. "Police department," he said. Then a moment later, "Lieutenant Madigan, please."

Madigan came on almost immediately. "Lieutenant Madigan talking."

"Your assistant, Johnny Fletcher. Look, who's your Number One candidate for the Soderstrom-Craddock killing?"

"The police department doesn't give out information," Madigan retorted. "And what's the idea asking such nonsense?"

"Oh, I wanted to tell you that if it

wasn't Matt Boyce, you're wrong."

"What's that, Fletcher?"

"Soderstrom wasn't murdered by Boyce."

"He'll have a chance to prove that. Say — what're you driving at?"

"I'm in Boyce's apartment. Boyce is here . . . but he's dead."

"Don't leave there!" Madigan howled.

Johnny hung up and looked at Jefferson Todd. "He says *no* one's to leave until he gets here."

"So you're going to drag me in," Todd said, glowering. "I'll remember that."

"So will I." Johnny sought out a couch and plopped himself down on it. "May as well be comfortable while waiting. Tell us about some of your big cases, Jefferson."

Jefferson Todd wasn't in a reminiscent mood, however. He paced the big living room like a caged animal. Johnny almost heard the swishing of a tail as Todd made the turns.

The wait wasn't a long one. In less

than ten minutes Lieutenant Madigan burst into the room, followed by a horde of men with cameras and equipment. Madigan gave Johnny just one dirty look on his way to the bedroom.

He remained in the room for more than five minutes, then came out and walked slowly up to Johnny. "Talk," he said, curtly.

"Talk? Sure. I love to talk. Did you ever hear the one about the real estate man's son who traded two five-thousand dollar cats for a ten-thousand dollar dog — "

"Cut it!" Madigan snarled. "I'm using sheer will power now to keep from dragging you down to the clink. How'd you happen to be here?"

Johnny produced the telephone message slip that Eddie Miller had given him at the 45th Street Hotel. Madigan gave it a quick glance. "You could have written this yourself."

"Not at the 45th Street Hotel. They don't like me that well there.

What's the time on it?"

"Three five. Where were you at that time?"

"In a book store on Fortieth Street, I can prove it."

"You'll have to . . . How long, Doc?"

A man with a black bag had come out of the bedroom. "Between two hours and two hours and fifteen minutes."

"Three o'clock?"

"Within a few minutes either way."

Lieutenant Madigan tapped the telephone message slip. "Just after he made this call. Or before. Maybe it wasn't Boyce who made the call at all."

"Clever of you to figure that out, Lieutenant," Johnny said, drily. "The murderer wanted the body discovered around five, so he sent messages to Todd and me."

"Todd? You get one, too?"

Jefferson Todd nodded unhappily. "The call came into my office a few minutes after three. But listen,

Lieutenant, I believe you should check into everyone's alibi — "

"I'm going to. Where were you at three o'clock, Todd?"

Todd's face twisted angrily. "As a matter of fact, I was talking to Mrs. Boyce at that moment."

"Ah, Mrs. Boyce!"

Johnny winked at Madigan. "Nice, gives Lulu an alibi. I wonder how much she inherits. Mmm, maybe baby comes home to papa, after all."

"What the devil are you talking about, Fletcher?"

"Oh, I was just thinking out loud. Sort of rumor I heard a while ago."

"About Lulu Boyce? Only eighteen columnists have printed that she and her husband parted."

"So? But she was still Mrs. Boyce."

"All right, she was. Now what about that baby-coming-home-to-papa gag?"

"What about it?"

"Don't get me sore, Fletcher."

Jefferson Todd sniffed. "He means Dan Murphy and Mrs. Boyce. Murphy claims Boyce cheated him out of the business. I doubt if she'll marry Murphy. I had a good talk with her this afternoon. She was using Murphy to make Boyce jealous. Actually, she was still in love with her husband."

"Holy pink elephants!" Johnny exclaimed.

Todd looked coldly at Johnny. "I happen to be an excellent judge of character."

"Phooey," cut in Sam Cragg.

"Remember, we're gentlemen," Johnny said, mockingly. "And Mrs. Boyce is a lady — with a million bucks."

"Fletcher," said Lieutenant Madigan, "will you do me a great big favor?"

"Anything, Maddy, old boy, Just name it."

"Then shut that big mouth of yours and take it away from here."

Johnny winced. "You don't want me to help you with this case?"

"Yes. But you can help best by getting the hell out of it. Go peddle your books and — "

"I can take a hint!"

Johnny held up a finger to Sam Cragg. "Come, Samuel!"

They left Matt Boyce's apartment, descended the flight of stairs to the elevator and rode down. In the lobby they encountered Ken Ballinger and Harry Hale just coming in. Johnny nudged Sam.

"Hi, fellows, what's new?"

Harry Hale was supporting Ken Ballinger by an arm — as usual. He gave Johnny a frosty grin. "I hear you're gumshoeing."

"Blockhead," Ken Ballinger said, thickly. "I know a guy could knot you into a pretzel."

"Bring him on," Sam invited cheerfully. "I'll let you hold one of my arms."

"Going up to see your boss?" Johnny asked innocently.

"Ken is," Hale said. "I'm just going along for the laugh. Ken's going to quit his job."

"Damn right I am," Ken retorted.

"I'm going to tell him all the things I been thinking for the last year."

"That'd be interesting. But Matt won't be listening, I'm afraid."

"He'll listen. I know things that'll make him listen."

"Such as what?"

"Hey," exclaimed Harry Hale. "What're you driving at, Fletcher?"

Johnny nodded toward the door. "Didn't you see all those cops out there? What do you think they're doing here?"

The owlish expression remained on Ken Ballinger's face, but Harry Hale gasped. "Matt . . . ?"

"Bingo!"

"I don't believe it."

"I found him myself," said Johnny, "and when I find them they're really dead. Run upstairs, though. It'll save Lieutenant Madigan the trouble of looking for you. Well, be seeing you."

Johnny passed out of the apartment house. Fifty feet from the building he said to Sam Cragg, "Those gold dust twins are pretty good actors. Particularly Ken."

"Huh, you think they knew?"

"If you're going to quit a job, do you wait until it's five o'clock and then go to your boss's home to tell him? I like to see people's faces when they're told their deadliest enemy has just been knocked off. I think we'll run over to the hotel and break the news to Jill Thayer."

"Jill? Heck, Johnny. She's a nice doll. I like her."

"So do I. That's why I want to help her out of this mess . . . Taxi!"

Ten minutes later Johnny paid off the taxi in front of the 45th Street Hotel and entered.

Peabody, the manager, was behind the desk. He smirked nastily as he regarded Johnny's new suit. The latter waved at him. "Nice, eh, Peabody?"

"Quite!"

They rode upstairs to the eighth floor, but at the door of Room 821 Johnny left Sam. "Be with you in a minute." He trotted down to the seventh floor and approached the door of 721. He listened for a moment, then knocked. There was no response and he tried the doorknob. The door was locked.

He went to the door of Room 717 and repeated the procedure, with similar results. Frowning he returned to Room 821. "Neither of them are home, Sam. I wonder . . . " he scooped up the telephone. "Eddie Miller, the bell captain."

A moment later Eddie Miller's cheerful voice said in his ear, "Ice water, chief?"

"Maybe later. What time did Miss Thayer leave the hotel, Eddie?"

"Yes," replied Edddie.

"Yes, what?"

"Yes, she left the hotel."

"All right, wise guy. I know she left the hotel. Did you see her leave?"

"Yes."

"What time was it?"

"I'm just trying to think."

"Cut it out," Johnny snarled. "You're not going to shake me down for every little thing."

"Why, I wasn't trying to shake you down, Mr. Fletcher. But things are slack and a guy's got to try to earn an honest dollar."

"No dollar you ever made was honest, Eddie. Now, come through or I'm going to get me a new stooge."

"Okay, Mr. Fletcher. They left the hotel about two thirty."

"They?"

"Her and this Tom Johnson. If I had a buck I could bribe the hack driver to tell me what depot they went to."

"Depot!" cried Johnny. "They didn't check out?"

"Johnson did, but Miss Thayer's keeping her room. She only took one bag."

"I'll be right down," said Johnny. He slammed the receiver on the hook and, looking at Sam, inhaled deeply. "I think things are moving, Sam!"

"I think Johnson's a punk," Sam said

disdainfully. "What she sees in him."

"I'll be right back."

Johnny darted out of the room and waited impatiently for the elevator to come up after he had pushed the button. When it finally came he stepped into the car and snapped. "All the way."

He found Eddie Miller talking to the doorman. The bell captain grinned. "I was just asking Carlo if he saw who the hack driver was?"

"Who was it, Carlo?"

The doorman screwed up his face and Johnny, groaning, took a dollar from his pocket. "All right, I know you're going to split. Who was it?"

"Bill Carnofsky. That's him right over there in the Yellow."

Johnny ran to where the taxi was parked a short distance from the hotel. He took a dollar from his pocket and waved it under the taxi driver's nose.

"A sweet-looking honey blonde, and a young squirt a couple of years younger; they had bags and you picked them up at the hotel at two-thirty. Where do you take them?"

The taxi driver picked up his chart. "Yeah, uh-huh, I drove them, but it's against the rules to tell."

"I know it is, but why do you think I'm waving this buck at you."

"No," said the hack driver. "I won't be dishonest for a buck. Make it two."

"It isn't worth it."

"This is, because I didn't take them to any hotel and it was such a long haul you'd never guess."

"Long haul? You mean the airport?"

"Hey!" cried the cab driver in chagrin."

Johnny put away his bill. "Stay honest, wise guy!" He went back to the hotel and caught hold of Eddie Miller. "No more cracks now, Eddie. This is serious. I like you and I'm going to do something for you, sometime. What do you really know about Jill Thayer and Tom Johnson?"

Eddie sighed. "They didn't act like

it. It was her and Ken Ballinger all the time. Johnson was younger than her, anyway. I wouldn't be a bit surprised if he was her kid brother."

Sam Cragg stepped out of the elevator and came over. "What's this all about, Johnny?"

"How should I know? No one ever tells me anything. Run upstairs and pack our bags."

"We've only got one."

"Well, pack it. Throw in our toothbrushes and your other shirt. We're taking a little trip."

"But your room rent's paid, Mr. Fletcher," said Eddie Miller. "Peabody won't give you a rebate."

"He would if I had the strength to argue the matter long enough. But I'll just have to take the loss. We'll hold the room as I expect to be back in a couple of days."

"Oh, you're not going very far?"

"No, not very far. Come, Sam."

In the elevator, Sam asked, "Where are we going, Johnny?"

"Just a little trip." Johnny winked and nodded at the elevator operator. In their room he finished. "We're going to Iowa."

"Iowa! Holy smokes! What do you want to do out there?"

"Get a copy of a high school paper." Sam gasped. "Are you nuts, Johnny?"

"I sometimes wonder. But a couple of people have been killed over that little paper."

"You're kidding!"

"I hope I am. But I don't think so. Come on, we're grabbing a plane."

And so they did. It got them into Chicago at one in the morning. There Johnny learned that the plane for Iowa would not be leaving until six in the morning so he and Sam went downtown to a hotel and caught a few hours' sleep. They were back at the airport at a quarter to six and fifteen minutes later were taking off for Waterloo, Iowa, almost three hundred miles due west.

14

THERE wasn't much at the little airport in Waterloo, when Johnny Fletcher and Sam Cragg descended from the big airliner.

"Cripes, there isn't even a burg here," exclaimed Sam.

"Oh yes, there is," Johnny replied. "It's hiding there behind that tree."

But a few minutes later when they were in the airport limousine which was taking them into the city they discovered that Waterloo was quite a bustling little city. The hotel to which they were taken would have done credit to a much larger city.

A bellboy took in their bag, but Johnny did not register at once.

"Where's Shellrock?" he asked the bellboy.

The boy shook his head. "What is it?"

"Ha-ha, a town. They told me it wasn't so far from here."

"I'll ask the clerk. He's an oldtimer around here."

The bellboy went into a huddle with the room clerk, which resulted in the latter producing a large-scale map. "Sh, yes," he said, "here it is. Mmm, I guess the best way to get to it is to take Highway 218 to Waverly, then the county road to Shellrock."

"How far is it?" Johnny asked.

"Twenty-two miles to Waverly — according to this map. Then six to Shellrock. Twenty-eight miles altogether."

Johnny scowled. "Isn't there a train goes there?"

"Oh, yes, but you've missed it for today. Be another one this time tomorrow. There's a train for Waverly in about four hours. I imagine you could take a taxi from there — if they have a taxi in Waverly. It's not much of a town."

"How about renting a car here?"

"Albert," said the clerk, "see if Philip is outside."

The bellboy went out of the lobby and returned after a moment with a man wearing a shabby suit and a cap with a cracked visor.

"Shellrock, Mister? I can get you there in an hour."

"For how much?"

"Well, it's quite a stretch. Will you be wanting me to wait around while you take care of your business?"

"Yes, I may have to spend two or three hours there."

The taximan whistled. "I'll have to charge you for my time in that case. Let's see an hour's driving each way, say three hours' waiting . . . would a dollar and a half be too much for the whole job?"

"Philip," said Johnny, "I might even go up to a dollar seventy-five. Where is this chariot of yours?"

"Right outside, mister. You ready to start?"

"As soon as I check our bags."

Two minutes later Philip led them to a pile of tin and rubber held together with baling wire. Philip kicked it and it clanked. "Ain't much to look at, but she's got a beautiful motor."

"I'm sure of it," said Johnny. He opened the rear car door and it came off in his hands. He chucked it in cheerfully. "After you, Sammy."

Sam stepped into the car and let himself fall on the seat. Something broke underneath and fell to the pavement, but Philip didn't even bother to see what it was. He climbed behind the wheel, did things and the machine exploded. He shifted into gear with a horrible grinding and a moment later the car was tearing up the street at fifteen or sixteen miles an hour.

"First trip to Waterloo?" Philip asked cheerfully.

"First trip to Iowa," Johnny replied. "I've always been afraid of the Indians."

"Haw-haw, there ain't no Indians in Iowa. Ain't been none in years. Greatest farming and dairy country in the whole United States. This here is Black Hawk County and Shellrock is in Bremer County; the dairy spot of Iowa, they call it — which means the whole bloomin' country."

"Do tell," Johnny murmured. "The farmers must be rich around here." He slumped down in his seat, hoping his lack of interest would damn the monologue that was flowing from Philip. But it didn't. Philips kept on and on. He zoomed the car along the road at all of thirty-five miles an hour and in a half hour or so pointed out the high spots in the town of Waverly, where he turned left and soon took to an old-fashioned Iowa graveled road. He slackened speed on this to a careful twenty-six miles an hour and in ten or fifteen minutes made another left turn and cried:

"There she is, Shellrock! I ain't been here myself for some time, but the old town ain't changed none. She was here during the Civil War. Where was you wanting to go, gents?"

"The high school."

"That's her right over there. Brand new and a beauty, ain't she?"

Johnny regarded the brick building with some uneasiness. "It's very nice. Wait outside. You too, Sam."

He entered the school building and located the principal's office. The principal turned out to be a mild-looking man in his late fifties. Yes, sir, what can I do for you?"

"My name is Fletcher," Johnny said. "I'm a private investigator from New York."

"New York? Well!"

"I'm engaged in a rather peculiar mission. I want to obtain a copy of your high school paper. A certain issue, published in the year 1951."

The principal pursed his lips and slowly shook his head. "That may be a little difficult. You see, the school burned down the summer before last. That's why we have this new building."

"I was wondering about that. You

216

printed the paper here in the school?"

"Oh, no, that was done by a local printer. I meant all our files were completely destroyed. All our records — everything. They went back sixty years. A very regrettable accident."

"You mean you wouldn't even be able to tell me who the members of the class of 1951 were?"

"That's right. My predecessor, Dr. Barr — a very fine gentleman — was the principal at that time. He passed on eight years ago. Of course, many members of the class still live around here and it's possible you could reconstruct a complete list of the members by talking to one."

"Who, for example?"

"Offhand it would be hard to say. Let me see, that's twelve years ago. The members of the class would be about thirty now."

"Thirty?" Johnny's eyes widened.

"Well, between twenty-eight and thirty-one. Dan Kiermeyer is about that age. He runs the little hardware store right up the street. Why don't you talk to him?"

"I will and thank you."

Dan Kiermeyer was of the class of '53. "I missed a couple of years in school and I didn't graduate until I was almost twenty," he said. "My cousin Amos Kiermeyer was graduated in '51. He's got the barber shop now."

Amos Kiermeyer was a cheery, roly-poly young man. "Yep, I graduated from high school in 1951. They almost had to burn the school down to get me out, heh-heh!"

"The school did burn down."

"Yeah, but not until a couple of years ago."

"Was there a boy named Tom Johnson in your class?" Johnny asked.

"Tom Johnson? No. There was a Jackson, but his first name was Eric. Don't know where he is now."

Johnny frowned. "No Johnson? How about a girl named Jill Thayer?"

"No. Is she good looking?"

"Very. Well, how about Ken Ballinger?"

"Never heard the name. You sure you're in the right town?"

"I think so. You had a paper called the Shellrock *Hi-Way*, didn't you?"

"Yeah, that's right. I hardly remembered it, though. Wasn't much of a paper."

"You don't know who the editor was?"

"Uh-uh. It only came out once in a while."

"You wouldn't have a copy at home?"

"Heck, no. What'd I want to keep it for?"

"I don't know. I just thought you might."

"I don't even keep last week's newspaper. Say . . . you oughtta talk to Ned Lester. He's a guy saves everything. I bet he's got two hundred books in his place. And come to think of it he had something to do with the high school paper."

"He's just the man I want to see. Where'll I find him?"

Amos Kiermeyer chuckled. "Wouldn't be a bit surprised if Ned was the richest man in these parts. He sure makes plenty."

"Well, where is he?"

"You drive out of town here about a mile and a half, on the road to Waverly. You come to a filling station, with a red windmill. But you won't find Ned at the windmill. But you'll find him at the big place right behind the windmill. Tell him I sent you. He'll like that."

"Thanks."

Johnny returned to the taxi and found Philip, the driver, droning out a monologue to Sam Cragg who, fortunately, was asleep in the back seat and wasn't hearing a word. He woke up, however, when Johnny climbed in beside him.

"All finished?"

"I've just begun. Philip, old man, drive back to the Red Windmill filling station on the road we came in."

"The Red Windmill? Oh-oh!"

"You know it?"

Philip made a clucking sound with his mouth. "Everybody knows it. Folks all the way from Des Moines come up. Lots of Waterloo people drive out, but them as can afford it have their own cars and don't take taxis so I never was there myself. Like to see it, though."

"You will now. What is it?"

"Tch. Tch. A place. You know."

"Oh," said Johnny.

It was quite a place. He was surprised that he had missed it coming in to Shelrock. But not too surprised when he scrutinized it carefully. The Red Windmill filling station was somewhat weatherbeaten and not too freakish for a filling station. And since it was morning and there were no cars about he had overlooked the graveled drive that led up a low hill behind the filling station.

The top floor of a large, almost square building made of treated pine logs showed over the crest of the hill.

"Fill up with gas, Philip!" Sam Cragg

suddenly haw-hawed.

Philip grinned. "I hear that eight times a day, mister. You're payin' for the gas? About three-four gallons will hold me."

"Get five. I'll pay."

Johnny climbed out of the car and nodded to the filling station operator. "Ned Lester at home?"

The man shrugged. "Maybe. Pretty early. How many?"

"Five. Okay, Sam."

Johnny and Sam trudged up the graveled drive and reaching the crest looked down upon the immense log building. There was parking field beside it large enough to accommodate two hundred cars.

As they approached a man wearing a white apron came to the door and dumped out a pail of dirty water.

"Top of the morning," Johnny said cheerfully. "Ned up yet?"

"Depends. What're you selling?"

"Not a thing, my good man. Not a thing."

"Collector?"

"This is strictly a social call. Amos Kiermeyer sent me. He went to school with Ned."

"Insurance?"

"You give up hard . . . Hey, Ned!"

"Jeez!" cried the man with apron. "Don't do that. Ned won't like it."

"Then trot him out. I have things to ask him."

A man who was as big as Sam Cragg, but meaner looking, shoved open the door beside the man with the apron.

"What the hell you yelling about?"

"You Ned Lester?"

"Yes, and I don't need a damn thing today, see?"

"Oh-oh," said Sam Cragg. "A tough guy."

Ned Lester turned his eyes on Sam Cragg and sneered. "Tough enough, fellow. What do you want?"

"Amos Kiermeyer sent me here."

"Then you can go right back. Any friend of Amos' isn't a friend of mine."

"I guess I got a bum steer. All right,

Amos didn't send me. I came all by myself. All the way from New York."

"I'm surprised they ever let you cross the Hudson. What's your racket?"

Johnny smirked. Ned Lester glowered for a moment, then said, "Come on in."

Johnny and Sam followed Lester into an immense room that smelled of sawdust and stale beer. There were booths down two sides, tables in the center and an orchestra stand in the rear. But Lester pushed open a door on the side and led the way through a smaller room that had a row of slot machines down one side and a long, narrow table in the middle of the room.

"Some of the local yokels play parcheesi," Lester said over his shoulder.

Lester reached another door at the rear and pushing it open waited for Johnny and Sam. The latter looked longingly at the slot machines.

"Will you be needing me, Johnny?" he asked.

"Not if you stick to the dime machine."

Lester laughed shortly. "Save your money, sucker. These machines are throttled down to ninety-ten."

"Oh, I'll play just for fun."

"Your funeral," Lester looked inquiringly at Johnny "I didn't get your name?"

"Fletcher, John Fletcher. My friend is Sam Cragg."

"And you're what?"

Johnny winked. "Investigation." He walked into the room which was fitted up as an office.

Lester followed and closed the door. "A dick! All the way from New York. Not. F.B.I.? Or treasury?"

"Nope. Nothing serious. I understand you graduated from the Shellrock High School in 1952?"

"Did I? Why?"

"I don't know why. Amos Kiermeyer said — "

"That fewbrains! Before you go any further, I live here, but I don't like

Shellrock and Shellrock doesn't like me, see? I'm outside the town limits and my customers — and friends — don't come from Shellrock. I make them pay a cover charge to keep them away. There isn't a Shellrock yokel would shoot more than a quarter and I can't run this place with quarters. See?"

"I see. But you did go to the high school and you had something to do with the school paper."

"If it'll make you any happier, I was the editor. So what?"

"Now," said Johnny, we're getting somewhere."

"Where?"

"Down to business. You wouldn't by any chance have a copy of the June, 1952, issue of the school paper?"

Lester's upper lip curled. "No, and I never saved my dance programs either."

"Lester," said Johnny, "let's detour a minute. How come you ever stayed out here in the corn belt?"

"I'm doing all right. I got into the

tail end of things down in Des Moines in '54 and '55 and then I came back here. This place has its advantages, see. If you live in Des Moines or Sioux City or maybe Davenport and you have to take a business trip, your wife can't follow you here, see?"

"I see," said Johnny. "So back to the mines. You haven't got a copy of the June, 1952, school paper; but would you remember what was in it?"

"No. Why should I remember?"

"Because I'd pay a hundred bucks."

"You've got a hundred dollars?"

"Well, not with me," Johnny said cautiously. "But I could get it pretty quickly."

"When you do, come back."

Johnny hesitated. "I've got fifty with me."

"No dice."

"Suppose I said I've got the hundred?"

"Let's see it."

Johnny inhaled heavily. "You're being very difficult, Lester."

"It's too damn early in the morning

for nonsense. What the hell would you want to know what was in a kid's school paper, twelve years old? Why would you come from New York for that?"

Johnny shrugged. "I don't know."

"You mean you get me all curious and then you don't know?"

"I'm trying to find out, I think it means something important, but I don't know. Ever hear of anyone named Egbert Cradock, or Hal Soderstrom?"

"No."

"How about Ken Ballinger? Harry Hale? Well — Tommy Johnson?"

"Bingo! What about Tommy?"

Johnny sighed. "Hurray for our side. Tommy was a classmate of yours?"

"Hell no, there was a kid by that name worked here a couple summers ago. He was only a punk."

"He didn't go to school with you?"

"Nah, he couldn't be more'n twenty-three, twenty-four right now. He didn't come from around here."

"From where did he hail?"

Lester shrugged. "How should I know? He bussed tables, but he wasn't any good at that because he was always hanging around in the — well, in another room. I gave him a chance there until he got molasses on his fingers. Then kicked him out."

"Molasses, eh? You mean he got sticky fingers?"

"All right," Lester growled. "You're smart enough. You got to trust a stickman, see? You can't watch them every minute. I check them in and out, but customers throw them a chip now and then when they have a lucky streak. Johnson got too many chips. He could palm them better than a magician."

Johnny screwed up his mouth. "But what did he know about the Shellrock High School paper?"

"Not a thing. Did he have to?"

"Yes. He fits into this somewhere."

"He fits into what?"

"Murder."

"Murder! Hey . . . get the hell out of here. I don't want any murder stuff around here. I can fix a squawk, or something, but not murder. Beat it."

"This murder happened in New York."

"Just the same, it can't walk in here. Sorry I even talked to you." Excitedly Lester took hold of Johnny's arm and began pulling him toward the door. Before they reached it, the door was kicked open and Sam Cragg plunged in.

"Okay, Johnny?"

"No," snapped Lester. "Scram outta here, the both of you."

Sam searched Johnny's face. "Yes or no?"

"Yes, I guess." Johnny replied. He shrugged his arm free of Lester's grip. "I hope all your help get glue on their fingers."

Lester sneered. "It won't be your dough."

Reluctantly Johnny left the roadhouse and walked back to the Red Windmill filling station. "You didn't make out, Johnny?" Sam asked.

"Not very well. But the damn thing's around here somewhere. For a minute I thought I had it. Well, we'll have to try elsewhere. All set, Philip?"

"Yep," said the taximan. "I got five gallons, but the danged stuff is two cents a gallon more'n it's supposed to be. He wouldn't take the gas out after he once put it in."

"S'all right. I'll pay for it. Back to Shellrock."

"Shellrock? Gosh, gee, it's twelve o'clock and I always go home for dinner. M'wife'll be worried about me."

"On second thoughts," said Johnny, "it's Waterloo I want to go to."

15

WHEN they were back in the car, Sam was silent for a moment, then heaved a tremendous sigh. "Did you get thrown for a loss by that guy, Johnny? Say the word and — "

"No, I don't think he knew. I should have worked the Waterloo angle first, anyway. Remember, back there in the bookshop in New York? Hochmeyer said he got the paper from a dealer named Langford in Waterloo . . . "

"Langford?" exclaimed Philip, the driver. "You mean Abe Langford?"

"Does he run a bookstore?"

"Yeh, two ways. He sells books and he makes book. Heh-heh-heh! Now it's been a quiet morning and I've had lots of time to think and the more I think about it the more I'm sure that Mad Mink will win in the third at Arlington.

I think I'll put a buck on her."

"A whole dollar?"

"Well, Langford won't take less'n a buck, but I always get Morris Balsington to put up a half with me. Yes, I think I can find him just in time. You fellows want to risk a dollar between you, Mad Mink's the name. Tell Abe I sent you and it'll be all right."

"Better yet, take us there and we'll put up a buck with your own."

"That's a bet, Mister. Hold your hats now, because I want to get there in plenty of time."

"Let 'er roll!"

Philip let her out. The car was screaming along at forty-two on the next straightaway and took the curves at better than thirty-five, so it wasn't more than an hour from Shellrock before Philip brought the jalopy up panting before a little bookstore a half block from the Russell Lamson Hotel.

The store was lined with shelves of books and had a couple of counters in the center heaped high with old volumes being offered five for a dollar. In the rear was a huge black tent with a knob on top of it. At least it looked like that to Johnny at first. Then the tent moved and he saw that it was a man; a man weighing over three hundred pounds and not more than five feet two inches tall.

It took him a long time to turn around and when he did, Johnny saw that someone else was standing behind him. Tommy Johnson, late of the 45th Street Hotel in New York.

"Hi, Abe!" called Philip, the cab driver. "Got a little business for you."

"We were going to place a bet," said Johnny Fletcher, "but never mind now. Hello, Tommy Johnson."

"The name is Smith," Johnson said curtly. "John Smith. Goodbye, Mr. Langford. If you find that book drop me a note."

Sam Cragg stepped in front of Tommy Johnson, but Johnny waved him aside. "Let him go, Sam."

"What can I do for you gentlemen?" the fat book dealer asked in a wheezing voice.

"Mad Mink in the third at Arlington," said Philip. "These gents and I want to lay it on the line; a dollar and a half all told."

"You've got the wrong place," said Langford. "I sell books, but I don't make them."

"Heh-heh-heh," chortled Philip. "I told these gents that joke. They laughed fit to kill."

"As a matter of fact," said Johnny, "Hockmeyer of New York gave me your name. I'm making a collection of high school papers of the early fifties. I need a copy of the Shellrock *Hi-way* to fill up my Iowa set. I understand you recently got one for Hockmeyer."

"Did I? I don't remember, but if he says so, I guess I did. Finding rare and out-of-print items is my business. You want I should look around for that paper? What was the name of it again?"

"Shellrock *Hi-way*, the same one Tom Johnson just talked to you about. The fella who just left."

"Him? He said his name was Smith."

"Johnson is just as phoney, so it doesn't make any difference, really. You can get the paper for me?"

"It'll cost money. It's really rare on account of the school burning down and the printer having gone out of business."

"I missed him," said Johnny, "so I saved a little time. I'll give you twenty-five dollars."

"Cost you fifty."

"When can you get it?"

"Tomorrow."

"You mean you know where one is?"

Langford nodded.

"Then why not get it today?"

"Can't."

"Look," said Johnny, "I came all the way from New York to get that paper. It's important that I get back. I'll give you ten dollars extra if you get it for me today."

Langford's fat cheeks puffed and he exhaled heavily. "It means a long trip and I don't travel so good. I've put on a little weight lately . . . "

"Yes, you *are* a little plump. You'll get it today then?"

"Tonight, I'll have to drive to Shellrock."

"It's only one o'clock. Why wait until evening?"

"Because I have an important out-of-town buyer coming here at three o'clock."

"Maybe I could go for the paper?"

"That's out of the question."

"Why, I'd see that you got your money, if that's what's worrying you."

"Well, it is. Naturally, I make a profit on a deal."

"Good, I don't care if you're getting the paper for nothing. You'll still get your sixty. Tell me where the paper is and I'll get it."

Langford hesitated. "Pay me the money."

Johnny took a roll of bills from his

pocket and counted out sixty dollars. Langford took the money and lumbered to a high writing stand. Leaning over he scribbled on a sheet of paper and folded it.

"You go to the Red Windmill in Shellrock — "

"The Red Windmill!" cried Sam Cragg.

Langford nodded. "I told you it was complicated. You've got to be cautious. There's a man there named Clem Meeker. Be sure you don't let anyone else know what you're there for. Give this to Clem Meeker and he'll give you the paper."

"Check," said Johnny. "And if I don't get it . . . ?"

"You'll get it."

"But if I don't . . . ?"

"Then I'll give you your money back."

Johnny hesitated, then nodded. "It's a deal."

"What about our'n?" Philip cried.

"All right, Philip," Langford said.

"You can pay me tomorrow."

"You mean I'll collect tomorrow."

Outside the bookstore, Johnny Fletcher said to the taxi driver. "Do you have to go home for lunch?"

"Uh-huh, I'm late now. Catch the dickens."

"All right, go ahead then. But pick us up at the hotel in a half an hour. We're going back to Shellrock. Here's three dollars which pays for the trip and the gasoline you bought . . . and a little over. I'll give you another three dollars for the next trip."

"You mean that, Mister? Then I'll sure pick you up."

"Good, We'll walk to our hotel. I see it right over there."

The moment they started walking, Sam Cragg exclaimed, "I don't like going back to that Red Windmill, Johnny."

"Why? How much did you lose?"

"Only about forty-five cents. It ain't that. It's . . . well, what did he write in the note?"

Johnny unfolded it and read:

Clem: Give bearer the other copy of the school paper. Same price. I'll send your money tomorrow, Langford.

"Nothing wrong with that," Johnny said.

"No, but this Johnson kid; where does he fit in?"

"Right in the middle. If he's here, Jill Thayer's here. They left New York together."

"Hey! That's right. And — jeez, Johnny! There she is!"

They were fifty feet from the hotel. Ahead, just entering, was Jill Thayer. Johnny made a sudden leap forward.

"Jill!" he cried. "Jill Thayer."

She whirled and her face twisted in consternation. For a moment it appeared that she was going to dart into the hotel, but then she slumped and waited for Johnny to come up.

"What are you doing here?" she asked.

"Same as you."

"You don't know why *I'm* here."

"Don't I?"

"No. This happens to be my home town. I came here for a visit."

"What a coincidence! I'm a native of Cedar Falls myself. Maybe we even went to the same school together. Mmm, maybe the Shellrock High School?"

"She blinked in annoyance. "Where are all your policemen friends?"

"I left them in New York. But that Lieutenant Madigan's a smart bird. And did that long-legged Jefferson Todd run you down before you left?"

"I don't know him."

"Then let me tell you about him." Johnny took Jill's arm. "Weren't you about to go into the cocktail lounge and have a drink?"

"I wasn't, but — "

"Fine. You remember Sam Cragg?"

"Blockhead, I believe."

"Hey," protested Sam.

"Sorry."

They went into the hotel and proceeded to the cocktail lounge, where Jill ordered a daiquiri. Johnny chose a dry martini and Sam a Pink Lady.

"Now," said Johnny, "we're both working the same side of the street, so why don't we compare notes? You're after a copy of the Shellrock High School paper. Why?"

"Don't you know?"

"Of course."

"Then why ask?"

Johnny cleared his throat. "You know about Matt Boyce, I suppose?"

"I read it in a Cleveland paper we took on when we landed there. Horrible. Who do you suppose . . . ?"

We're clear," said Johnny. "but I think Lieutenant Madigan wanted to check *your* alibi."

"That's absurd. I had no dealings with the man. My dislike for him was secondhand, because of Ken Ballinger."

"What about Tommy Johnson?"

The color was suddenly drained from her cheeks. "What . . . about . . . who?"

"Tommy Johnson. He's probably up in his room right now. I saw him only ten minutes ago, in the bookstore."

Jill Thayer looked steadily at Johnny for a moment, then the tip of her tongue came out and moistened her lips. "All right, Tommy told me he'd surprised you in my room in New York. But what do you know about him?"

"Your brother?"

"Cousin. Tommy's always been interested in drawing and when he came to New York he looked me up. He needs instruction and I've been giving it to him."

"Isn't he good enough to draw comics?"

"If the art editor isn't too particular. He'll be better in three or four months. He knows it."

"Where did he go to school?"

"Des Moines, then Iowa City. The State U."

"What's he done between school and now?"

Jill became annoyed. "What's this, a third degree?"

"No. Sorry. I got started on this and I'm trying to tie up a lot of ends."

"Why? Jill sighed wearily. "I asked you the same question in New York. You can't get anything out of this."

"What can *you* get out of it?"

She suddenly picked up her purse and pushed back her chair. Johnny held out his hand to stop her. "Wait a minute. Answer just one question then I won't bother you any more."

She got up and looked down at him. "The answer is no."

"But I didn't ask the question — and it doesn't require a yes or no. What's in that school paper?

"The answer is still no. And now if you'll excuse me I'm late for luncheon with my grandfather." And with that she swept out of the cocktail lounge.

A waiter came up with a check. Johnny winced and paid it, but neglected to add a tip, thereby receiving a scowl. As they left the room he said to Sam:

"Philip's going to get a standoff this afternoon. That brought the bankroll down to two dollars and fourteen cents."

"What!" cried Sam in horror. "I thought we were holding heavy."

"We were — in New York. But our airplane tickets out here and the sixty bucks for the book . . . How much money have you got?"

Sam reached into his pocket and brought out a dollar bill and two nickels. "A dollar ten, that's all."

"So we've got three twenty-four. If we pay Philip we'll have twenty-four cents left over."

"He really only wanted a buck and a half. And you already overpaid him."

"So I did. Well, give me your dollar and I'll see how far I can stretch it."

"Put some rubber in it, Johnny. Holy smoke!" Sam groaned. "I'm always scared stiff when we're broke away from New York. There I don't mind it so much, because you always manage to get us a stake somehow. But in a burg like this — "

"We've been all around the country and you haven't starved yet, have you?"

"No, but I've missed some meals. And you know I like my food. That reminds me, we haven't had lunch."

"The Pink Lady was your lunch. It costs fifty cents. I think Philip is waiting for us."

He was. And very cheerful about it. "Ah, there you are, gents. I was afraid you'd run out on me. Glad you didn't. She's sure a lucky day for me. Two long trips like this'n . . . "

"And don't forget Mad Mink," said Johnny. Well, let's away."

16

THE return trip to the Red Windmill was made without incident, if you discounted Philip's monologue. They left Philip at the filling station and walked to the roadhouse, which now had eight or ten cars parked beside it.

They entered and found a half dozen customers at the bar. The big waiter who had poured out the dirty water that morning was behind the bar.

"Back, huh?" he grunted as he came up behind the bar.

"You've got good beer here. How about a couple of schooners, Bill."

"The name ain't Bill."

"No? What is it?"

"Bartender. Two beers coming up."

He went off and drew the beer, but when he came back, Johnny said, "You know you look like your name might be Clem."

"It is, but — say, what is this?"

"Shh!" said Johnny. "I've got a note for you. From Abe Langford."

Clem Meeker's eyes slitted. "Let's see it."

Johnny took it out of his pocket, along with a dollar bill to pay for the drinks. He put both on the bar. Clem picked up the two pieces of paper, took one to the cash register and got change. Returning with the change he dropped a quarter on the floor and stooped to pick it up. It took a moment to find it. When he brought the change to Johnny his face was red.

"I can't now. You'll have to come back tomorrow."

"If I could have waited until tomorrow Abe Langford would have got it for me. I need it today, right now."

"But I can't get it. The boss — "

"What about him? Is it in his office?"

"Not exactly . . . is there anything else, gents?"

The quick change in Clem Meeker's

tone caused Johnny to scoop up his glass of beer, Tilting it to his mouth he looked into the back-bar mirror and saw Ned Lester coming up. He put down the glass, turned casually, then beamed.

"Hi, Neddy!"

"You," scowled Lester. "Didn't I tell you to keep away from here?"

"This is pleasure, Lester."

"Drinking a glass of beer? You can get beer anywhere."

"Not as good as this. Besides," Johnny winked, "thought there might be something doing about now."

Lester hesitated, then nodded. "There is."

"Swell! Lead on . . . " As he turned away, Johnny winked at Clem the bartender. Then he followed Ned Lester to the door of the gambling room.

There were eight or ten men around the crap table, an elaborate affair with ridged, rubber sideboards and betting squares stenciled on the felt table cloth.

A man with a stick stood behind the table. Before him were stacks of silver dollars and large, yellow chips.

"And the gentleman sevens out," he announced as Johnny came up.

Ned Lester caught the eye of the stickman. "Here're a couple of gentleman want action."

"We'll try to please," the stickman said, smiling mechanically. "Next gentlemen one yellow to pass."

Johnny and Sam took places at the table. The man who had the dice shook them up and threw them against the rubber sideboard. They came up on eight and he placed a yellow chip on the line beside the first one.

"Five to eight," the stickman droned.

The shooter threw out the dice again and they stopped on seven. The stickman snaked in the pair of yellow chips. "Next gentleman."

"I shoot a quarter," said Johnny.

Every eye in the room, with the exception of Sam Cragg's came toward Johnny. The stickman said politely,

"We use silver dollars for chips and the yellow chips are five dollars."

"Ha, ha," said Johnny. "I was kidding, I shoot a dollar." He knew very well that he had exactly two dollars and ninety-four cents on his person. And Sam Cragg had two nickels. But he put a dollar on the pass line.

"You're off," said the stickman.

"Wait a minute," said one of the other players. "A new man's always lucky. Two yellows he passes."

Johnny took up the large green dice that the stickman shoved to him, shook them up and rolled them out. They bounced off the rubber and came back half-way across the able.

"Ace-deuce," said the stickman, politely. "Crap."

"Jeez!" groaned Sam Cragg.

"Always double after a crap," said the man who had lost two yellow chips on Johnny. He put out four yellows.

Johnny stuck his finger under his collar and loosened it. "I never double on crap." He put out his sole remaining dollar bill.

"Tsk. Tsk," said Ned Lester at Johnny's elbow. "I thought you wanted action."

"I play hunches," said Johnny. "I'm off with a beautiful natural."

"Ten," said the stickman. "We lay two to one on ten."

"I'll take four yellows worth of that," said the man who was riding with Johnny. He put out his chips.

Johnny grinned. "I won't spoil your luck by betting with you. But there she come — right back."

"Seven," said the stickman. "The house wins. Next man."

"Me?" said Sam Cragg. "Uh-uh."

"Shoot," said Johnny. "Here, I'll give you some chicken feed. We'll jinx the house with it." He brought out the ninety-four cents from his pocket, put back the four pennies and handed the balance to Sam. The latter fished out his two nickels and grinned uneasily.

"The works," he said and put it all on the pass line.

The stickman caught Ned Lester's eye. The latter muttered under his breath. Then he laughed shortly. The gamekeeper raked in the small change with his stick and substituted a silver dollar.

"I'm off," said the man who had lost six yellow chips on Johnny.

Sam Cragg closed his big fist on the dice, shook them up and hurled them against the backboard. They bounced clear back, hitting the near end broad.

"Eleven," said the stickman and dropped a silver dollar on top of Sam's.

"Shoot it," said Johnny.

Sam did and came up with a four and a three. "Let it ride," Johnny advised.

The player who had been with Johnny put out a yellow chip, then snatched it back. "He can't make a third pass."

But Sam did. The gamekeeper added

four dollars more to the pile.

"I pinch seven," Sam declared.

"Don't be a fool," Johnny exclaimed. "You can make another pass."

Sam frowned, but let the money remain on the table. He promptly threw another seven and yelled, "Wowee!"

Eight silver dollars joined the eight on the table. "All of it," Johnny said.

"That's foolish," said the outside player. "Nobody's made five passes today."

"Sam can do it. Go ahead, Sam." Sam shook up the dice and then stopped on Little Joe — four.

"I told you," said the kibitzer.

"Don't bet on the four, Sam," said Johnny "You'd jinx it."

"Yeah, I know, said Sam, discouraged. "I shouldda pinched." He rolled out the dice and they stopped at three-on.

"Holy Moses!" Sam cried.

"All of it," exclaimed Johnny. "Thirty-two pounds of silver."

"Sorry, gentlemen," said the stickman.

"The house limit twenty-five dollars. You'll have to draw down seven dollars."

"What?" cried Johnny. "You've got a limit? Hell, we wanted action."

"I'm sorry, twenty-five is the limit per play. You can bet the same amount on a point, or a come bet, but twenty-five is the limit."

"Just for that," said Johnny, "shoot a dollar, Sam."

"Can't he think for himself?" Ned Lester snarled.

"Pull it down, Sam," Johnny said, pretending not to hear Lester.

Sam obeyed. "One buck is all I shoot."

"Mistake," said the player down the line. "You're hot. I lost money not riding with you, but I'll make up now. Five yellows he passes."

Sam threw a twelve and John chortled. "See? I could smell that crap."

"Goddamit," wailed the other crap shooter.

Johnny winked. "Jump aboard now, brother. We're going to pass three times since we got rid of that."

"No, I'm off for good."

"Then shoot the limit, Sam."

"Huh? Twenty-five bucks? That leaves only six — "

"Shoot twenty-five."

"Shoot," said the gamekeeper.

"You're through," Lester sneered.

Sam rolled out an eleven. Three players promptly showered money on the table. "He's really hot." But the man who had lost a small fortune on Johnny and Sam held back. "Not me; he's through."

"Twenty-five is the limit," cautioned the stickman. He put five yellows chips beside Sam's stack of silver dollars.

Sam took back his silver. "Okay, buddy, I'll play with your chips. One more natural . . . dammit, it's ten."

"Two to one on ten . . . "

"Take it, Sam. You're going to make it. You're hot!"

Two fives came up. Sam raked in

his own bet and fifteen yellow chips in addition. "You lucky stiff," Ned Lester said, bitterly. "You started with nothing but a bunch of chicken feed."

" . . . And we'll wind up with a poultry farm," said Johnny cheerfully. "The limit, Sammy, old boy."

Sam got four for a point, bet twenty-five that he would make it, then on Johnny's advice bet another twenty-five that he would 'come.' He got nine for a come point and bet twenty-five dollars that he would make it.

He made both points and collected ninety dollars in yellow chips (nine paid only forty to twenty-five). He then made two naturals and a point, after which he sevened out, losing the dice and having accumulated almost four hundred dollars in the ten minutes or so that he had held them.

"And now you can quit, you lucky stiff," Ned Lester growled.

"Quit? said Johnny. "hell, we're just starting."

"With my money."

"We've got plenty of our own, Mister."

"Yah! That's why you counted out pennies and nickels."

"A jinx bet, pure and simple," Johnny said loftily.

"And you wanted to start with two bits."

"Kidding," said Johnny. "Here, Sam, I don't want to break a bill. Lend me a few of those chips for a minute."

"Sure, Johnny, help yourself."

The man who had lost all the money on Johnny and Sam had the dice. "Five yellow I shoot," he said. "Since the dice are so hot maybe I can get back what I lost."

"Five yellows he dumps," said Johnny putting the chips on the no-pass line.

The man glared at him. "You think your pal took all the sevens off?"

"All but those he's going to make the next time around."

"Yah!"

The man shook up the dice and promptly threw a four, sevening out on the next roll. He cursed bitterly and Johnny collected five yellow chips along with his own.

The other players took their turns with the dice and Johnny bet against all of them. He won more than a hundred dollars before the dice came around to him. Feeling that his luck had turned he shot twenty-five dollars . . . and threw a crap.

"What kind of cheap joint is this?" he demanded loudly. "A man can't even double after a crap!"

Ned Lester tapped him on the shoulder. "For you, wise guy, I'll remove the limit."

"A piker fifty?" Johnny asked, curling his lips comtemptuously.

"Your bankroll, sport," snapped Lester. He nodded to the stickman. "And your fat friends's."

"Who you calling fat?" Sam demanded.

"You!" snarled Lester. "Now put up or shut up."

"We'll put up," said Johnny. "Sam, dump it all on the table."

"The silver too?"

"The silver too."

The stickman had finally lost his poise. He was biting his lips as he stacked up the yellow chips and the silver dollars to count them.

"I make it six-twenty-nine," he said after a moment or two.

"It rides," said Johnny. "And here I come with a nice big . . . "

"Seven!" cried everyone in the room.

"Seven," said Johnny softly. "Does it still ride, Mr. Lester?"

"No," Lester said, thickly. "The game's closed."

"Twelve-fifty-eight, Mr. Lester. And no checks, please."

"Come to my office," said Lester. "Leave the silver on the table. I'll give you the money in bills."

"Right-o!"

"Oh, mama, mama, papa!" Sam intoned reverently. "This never happened to me before."

"Tut-tut, Sam, have you forgotten when we broke the bank in Las Vegas?

And what about the time we nicked Nick for eighteen G's in Chicago?"

"When . . . ?"

"Ha ha!" laughed Johnny. "You're too modest. S'all right; Ned doesn't mind. He takes the guys for plenty here; he can afford to lose one time."

"Have your fun," Lester said, sourly. They had reached the office and he opened the safe. Removing a tin box he scooped out a double handful of large bills in packets. He tossed two packets on a table, then broke a third and counted off fourteen twenties. He took money from his pocket and added eighteen dollars.

"There you are, boys, it's all yours. Twelve hundred and fifty-eight bucks. I knew you were bad luck when you came in here his morning."

"Only twelve fifty-five of this is winners," Johnny said. "We risked three bucks of our own money."

"That makes a difference," Lester said sarcastically. "I don't feel so badly now. Well, it's been nice knowing you, goodbye and kindly forget my address."

"Oh, we wouldn't want to do that, Mr. Lester. But we do have to run. Mmm, a cold glass of beer, then home.

Lester remained in his office as Johnny and Sam passed out of the bar.

Clem Meeker signaled to Johnny even before he reached the bar. "I got it," he whispered hoarsely as he leaned over and polished the mahogany. "Gimme a bill and I'll give it to you with your change."

"Two nice cold beers," said Johnny.

He paid for the drinks with a five dollar bill and with the change received a thick, folded packet of paper. He stuck it in his trouser pocket, and quaffed the beer.

"Good beer," he said to Sam, "but I don't think we've got time for another."

"No," said Sam. "We'd better beat it."

They left the roadhouse and walked down to where Philip was waiting in his taxi.

"Back to Waterloo, Philip, and don't spare the horses."

"Heh-heh-heh," cackled Philip. "I been thinking bout horses. The third at Arlington ought to be over now; if Mad Mink didn't win I lost four bits."

"If you do, I'll pay your bet," Johnny said. "You've treated us swell and I'd like to do something for you."

"Say, you're really gents," Philip declared warmly. "Well, we're off for home."

A half mile from the Red Windmill there was a sharp turn in the graveled road. Around it a limousine was parked sidewise in the road.

17

JOHNNY groaned. "In broad daylight!"

Philip was braking the jalopy into the limousine, crumpling his own fenders but not doing much damage to the other car.

The two men who popped out from behind the touring car both had big automatics. "Up with 'em!" they cried.

"No!" cried Sam, hysterically. "I never won that much in my life and I ain't goin' to be robbed."

"Cousin," said one of the gunmen, "heaven's full of heroes. I ain't got blanks in this roscoe. See?"

He deflected the gun from Sam and fired at one of Philips's tires. The air went out with a hiss and whine.

"See what I mean?"

"All right, Sam," said Johnny hopelessly. "It wasn't in the cards

— I mean the dice. Give it up."

"That's what we want *you* to do, mister. Give it up."

Johnny started to reach for his breast pocket, but one of the gunmen leaped forward. "Hold it cousin, I'll get it." He circled Johnny and came up from behind. He thrust the muzzle of his automatic into Johnny's spine and snaked his free hand over Johnny's shoulder.

Sam chose that moment to make a leap for the second gunman. The hand over Johnny's shoulder was crooked and came up under Johnny's chin in a tight stranglehold. The automatic scraped his spine so viciously that Johnny cried out in pain.

Sam hit the gunman's hand at the exact instant that the man pulled the trigger. The bullet seared the calf of Sam's left leg. But he wasn't incapacitated. He gripped the gunman's wrist with his left hand and slapped it with his right. The automatic flew fifty feet away, landing somewhere in the bushes along the side of the road.

The man whose wrist Sam was holding cried out in pain. Sam cuffed him on the side of the head, knocking him to his knees.

Then a bullet tore through Sam's coat-tail and the man holding Johnny Fletcher cried out: "The next bullet goes through your head!"

Sam whirled, crouching, "Leggo, Johnny!" he cried hoarsely.

The man at his knees scuttled toward the car. Sam took a step forward. The automatic that had been in Johnny's spine barked again. Sam missed a step and fell forward on his hands and knees.

The automatic came back into Johnny's spine and the holder of it snarled into his ear. "Into the car, or I'll let him have it — where it hurts."

Raising himself to his haunches Sam saw Johnny piling into the car under the threat of the automatic. "Hold it, Johnny!" he cried.

He plunged toward the car, and at that instant it leaped away.

Sam screamed. "Stop, you dirty . . . !"

The car hit the embankment, made a wild screeching turn and tore off. Sam, bleeding from wounds in the thigh and calf, tried to limp after it, but it was no use.

He turned to meet Philip, who had gotten out of his own car. "I got their license number!" Philip exclaimed. "H-2755!"

"They got Johnny," Sam moaned, "If they hurt him, so help me, I'll tear off their arms and legs and beat out their brains with them. Get into that car and let's get after them."

"No use. They shot a tire and, mister, you're bleedin' all over. You're shot."

"Scratches," snapped Sam. "Change that tire and let's roll."

"Ain't got a spare. Can't afford it. But I can repair this one, First, lemme look at that leg o'yourn."

Impotent with rage, Sam seated

himself on the running board of the old flivver. Philip knelt before him and gently raised the trouser leg. He whistled. "The one in the calf is only a scratch, but the other . . . Mmm . . . "

"It doesn't hurt. Come on . . . "

"There's about an ounce of meat gone from your thigh. Bullet went clear through. That's lucky . . . "

"Lucky, hell!" Sam slipped a handkerchief from his pocket. "Tie this around it."

Philip made a clucking sound with his mouth. Then he folded Sam's handkerchief into a narrow pad and wrapped it round the thigh. He took out his own huge bandana and used it for a bandage to go over Sam's handkerchief.

"Maybe that'll hold until we get to the doctor."

"I haven't time for a doctor. Look, here comes a car . . . !"

It was a car almost as old as Philip's and was driven by a farmer in faded overalls and torn shirt. He was braking even before Sam started waving to him.

"Blowout?" he asked. "Can I help?"

"Yes," said Sam, "but first you can give me a lift — to the Red Windill."

"They went t'other way," Philip said.

"Maybe so, but they'll circle round the Red Windmill. Mister, did you meet a bus, license number H-2755?"

"Why, no, I didn't. Something wrong?"

"Nothing I can't handle. Come on, gimme that lift, mister."

The farmer looked inquiringly at Philip. The latter nodded. "If you could come back . . . "

"Sure, glad to help out. Okay, mister."

Sam got into the farmer's car and they started toward the Red Windmill.

"Look, mister," said the farmer, "You look like a stranger around here. If I was you I wouldn't do anything reckless at the Red Windmill. They're a bunch of highbinders there. There's talk that they run one of them there roulette wheels."

"I wouldn't know about roulette wheels, but chances are the Red Windmill is going out of business. About five minutes after I get there."

"Eh?"

"I'm going to wreck the place. There won't be a wall standing when I get through."

"Gee, mister, you don't want to try anything rough at the Red Windmill. August Kraft said they got bouncers there. And he oughtta know, seein's how he got bounced himself."

"Here's the joint," said Sam. "Thanks for the lift and if you could go back and help Philip — "

"Oh sure. I'll go right back!"

"Swell!"

Sam walked deliberately toward the Red Windmill filling station. Reaching it he stepped to one side and took hold of a red picket fence. He gave it a sudden wrench and broke down an entire section.

The filling station operator bounded out of the Red Windmill. "Hey, whaddya think you're doing?"

Sam ignored him. He ripped of pickets until he had cleared five feet of the two-by-four backing. Then he picked up one end and brought it down with a tremendous crash on top of one of the fence posts. A five-foot chunk of two-by-four broke out. He picked it up and turned toward the filling station man, who backed hurriedly into his hideout.

Without a word Sam walked past and climbed the knoll unmolested, kicked it open and entered the barroom.

Clem Meeker caught sight of him and winced noticeably, for Ned Lester was at the far end of the bar. Lester also caught sight of Sam.

"I thought I told you to stay away from here," he growled.

Sam walked across the floor to within a couple of steps of the bar. He grinned wickedly and raised his section of lumber. He brought it down upon the bar with all the strength in his tremendous shoulders.

The impact of the two-by-four upon the mahogany bar could have been heard in Shellrock, two miles away. The mahogany crashed and splintered under the blow.

Sam raised the two-by-four again, but held it over his head as he roared, "Shell out, Ned Lester, you dirty, sneaking, lying, cheating yellowbelly. Shell out that twelve-fifty-eight or so help me, I'll make matchwood out of your whole shebang."

Ned Lester, who had started toward Sam, had frozen. His eyes were bulging in horror and his lower jaw hung slack.

"What — what are you — trying to do?"

"Wreck the joint!" howled Sam Cragg. "And don't give me any of that innocent stuff. You know damn well you sent your gunmen out to hold us up. I got two bullets in me and they kidnapped Johnny Fletcher. Break him out or by God — "

"You're crazy!" Lester cried hoarsely. "I didn't — "

Crash!

The two-by-four came down again on the bar, ruining it utterly. For emphasis Sam whirled and completely demolished a table with a single blow. Then he advanced on Ned Lester.

"Come clean Lester, come clean. I'm going to count three and if you don't come clean by them, you're a dead man . . . ?"

"A wild-eyed man burst through the office door gripping a double-barreled shotgun.

"Shall I let him have it, Ned?" he cried.

"Yes!" thundered Sam. He hurled the two-by-four at the gunman as another man would throw a small stick. The man with the shotgun screamed — and then the gun roared.

Glass crashed as the charge blasted the back-bar mirror. A few wild pellets of lead stung Sam Cragg, but didn't deter him. He leaped forward, both arms flung out and enveloped Ned Lester in a mighty embrace.

Ned Lester cried out in terror and anguish. "Let me go, you wild man, let me go. I'll give you whatever you ask, but let me go."

Sam relaxed his embrace, but caught Lester by the shoulders and shook him until the roadhouse proprietor's teeth rattled. "To hell with the money. I want Johnny Fletcher."

"But I haven't got him," sobbed Lester. "I don't know what you're talking about."

The note of sincerity in Lester's hysteria penetrated Sam's fogged, enraged brain. He let go of Lester and peered into his face.

"Your gunmen didn't kidnap Johnny?"

"No, of course not. I don't even know what happened."

"Two guys with automatics and a car, licence Number H-2755 . . . they ain't yours . . . ?"

"No, of course not."

"Then who are they?"

"I don't know — wait! We'll call the State Motor Vehicle Department." Lester sprang to a wall telephone, tore down the receiver and cried, "Operator, give me the State Vehicle Department at Des Moines. No, I don't know the number. But hurry, this is an emergency. Ned Lester talking . . . "

He signaled to Sam who hurried over to the phone. It was less than thirty seconds before Lester snapped into the mouthpiece. "Motor Vehicle Department? Give me the commissioner. Tell him it's Ned Lester and hurry . . . Hello, Harold? This is Ned Lester. Do me a favor — quick. License Number H-2755 . . . what's the name and address? Right away, I'll hold on . . . You've got it right before you? . . . Repeat that, Harold . . . "

He thrust the receiver to Sam's ear and the latter heard a voice saying. "The car was reported stolen in Waterloo last night. It was found wrecked near Oelwein, but the plates were missing . . . "

"Thanks, Mister," said Sam Cragg and hung up.

Ned Lester looked bitterly at him. "Satisfied?"

"No, I won't be satisfied until I see Johnny — in the pink. But — but I guess maybe you didn't do it, after all."

"Damn right I didn't. And who's going to pay for the damages."

"Send me a bill," retorted Sam. "And if I don't pay it, sue me."

"Get out of here," Lester said thickly. "You've caused me enough damage for one day. Winning that money and then — this!"

The phone on the wall jangled. Sam had turned away when Ned Lester called him.

"Hey, you — big fellow. This call's for you."

Sam turned and saw Lester holding the receiver to him. "What? For me?"

"Your name's Cragg, isn't it? It's that wise pal of yours . . . "

"Johnny!" Sam bounded back toward

Lester and snatched the receiver from him. "Johnny!" he cried into the mouthpiece. "Jeez, Johnny, you all right?"

"I'm all right, Sam," said Johnny's cool voice. "I mean I'm not hurt, but — " Johnny's voice broke off and Sam screamed, "What is it, Johnny? For the love of Mike, talk . . . !"

Johnny's voice came on again. "As a matter of fact, Sam those — sh, boys are holding me. They say they're going to play rough with me."

"They hurt you they'll answer to me! Tell 'em to come to the Red Windmill and see what I done here. Tell'em that . . . "

"They haven't got anything to do with the Red Windmill," Johnny said, "But they — uh — they want that high school paper. You know, the . . . "

18

SAM blinked. "But Johnny, didn't they get it from you?"

"Well, no, Sam. They got the money, but not — that! Uh, I guess the game's up, Sam. I told them that you had it."

"But I haven't, Johnny . . . "

"Go back to the hotel in Waterloo, Sam. They'll telephone you there and tell you what to do. Get that, Sam? Go to the hotel and — "

The line went dead.

With a trembling hand, Sam put the receiver on the hook. Ned Lester who had been watching him, asked, "Something wrong with your pal?"

"No, nothing wrong." Sam moistened his lips with his tongue. "Nothin' at all. So long — I hope."

He was running by the time he reached the door and the most welcome sight he had seen in days was the ancient jalopy of Philip, just wheezing up to the filling station.

"Turn 'er around, Philip!" Sam cried. "We're headin' for Waterloo!"

"D'you telephone the cops?"

Sam bounced into the back of the car. "Yeah, they said to get right back to Waterloo." He thrust his hand down into the crevice back of the cushion. He found it almost immediately, an eight-page newspaper folded into a small packet. He opened it and read the title: Shellrock *Hi-Way*.

"So this is it," he muttered under his breath. "Now, I'll see what all the shoutin's about."

Most of the first page was devoted to last week's football game with the Waverly High School. Shellrock had won by the score of 128 to 7 and this was cause for much jubilation. Sam turned the page and read an announcement of the forthcoming school dance and a page of chatter concerning the activites of the various students.

He turned to page four and saw that the page was devoted to a badly drawn comic strip. He skipped it and went to page 5, adjoining. Then his eyes went back to the comic strip and he gasped. The title of the strip was 'Blockhead, the Strong Man' and the pictures depicted the adventures of a super Hercules. Sam's eyes shot up to the title again and he noted the legend after it: 'Drawn by Enoch Holtzman.'

"This is it!" Sam exulted.

Philip's head swiveled around. "You say somethin', mister?"

"Yeah, how far to Waterloo?"

"Not far, we just went through Cedar Falls. 'Bout five miles more. How d'you s'pose Mad Mink made out?"

"I don't know and I don't care."

"But, gosh, you got a buck on him!"

"And my pal's in a jam. He's worth more than a buck. Besides, he had twelve hundred and fifty-eight dollars on him."

"Twelve hundred — holy Angora cats!"

Philip jammed his foot down on the accelerator and the jalopy's speed leaped up to a perilous thirty-nine and forty. In a few moments if was careering around a corner into Waterloo and did not stop until it reached the hotel.

There, Sam Cragg reached into his pocket and winced. "Johnny'll pay you tomorrow, Philip," he said. "He's got all our dough. Uh, he'll include for the tire, too."

"Yeah, sure, but — " protested Philip, but Sam did not hear him. He was darting into the hotel and up to the desk.

"What room are Johnny Fletcher and myself in?" he cried.

"Don't you know?"

"No, we only checked our bag here this morning. We was figuring to get the room later."

"Oh, then I'll assign you one. Let's see, how about a nice double, with shower and tub — "

"Anything. Any old room at all."

"I see. Something about five dollars?"

"One buck, five, ten — anything, but hurry!"

"Very well — front! Mr. Cragg's bag . . . "

"Never mind the bag, the room . . . "

"Show the gentleman to 418."

Sam was in the elevator while the bellboy was still fumbling with the key. They rode up to the fourth floor and walked down a long corridor. The bellhop unlocked the door of Room 418, fussed with the windows and looked into the bathroom. "Shall I bring up your bags now, sir?"

"No, let it go for a while."

"Very well, uh, is there anything else?"

The bellboy began rubbing his hands together. Sam Cragg scowled and digging into his pockets brought out his entire wealth — four pennies. He gave them to the boy.

"Thank you, my boy."

The bellboy looked at the pennies. "What's this?"

Sam snarled and catching the bellboy

by the seat of his trousers and the scruff of his neck ran him out of the room. "I haven't time for any nonsense!"

The bellboy landed on his feet, running. Sam started to turn back into Room 418, then the door of Room 417 opened and he looked at Jill Thayer.

"Oh!" she exclaimed.

"Oh, yeah!" cried Sam. He suddenly caught the girl's wrist and jerked her into his room.

She screamed, "Let me go, you stupid blockhead."

"I haven't got time for games," Sam snapped. "Johnny Fletcher's been kidnaped and you're the cause of it."

"Kidnaped . . . what are you talking about?"

"As if you didn't know. We went to the Red Windmill near Shellrock and when we were leaving a couple of gunmen stuck us up."

"You're hurt!" Jill Thayer suddenly exclaimed.

"Me? Nah, just a couple of scratches. But they got Johnny. They're going to telephone here — "

"How do you know?"

"Because they said so. I went back to the Red Windmill to break it up and they telephoned me there. Said they'd telephone here and tell me where to bring the paper."

"What paper?"

Sam whipped it out of his pocket. "This. Didn't you get one yet? Cripes, it's what these guys want, to let Johnny go. But I don't get it. There ain't nothin' in here but a crummy cartoon about Blockhead — "

"Let me see it!"

Sam started to hand it to Jill, then was overcome by caution. "I'll hold it." He opened the Shellrock *Hi-Way* to page four and held it so Jill Thayer could see it.

She leaned forward a little. "Enoch Holtzman! but that's — that isn't . . . I mean . . . " her hand suddenly flew to her mouth.

"What do you mean?" Sam demanded.

"Nothing, I — where'd you get that paper?"

"From the barkeep at the Red Windmill. Didn't that punk cousin of yours get himself one?"

Jill's sharp, white teeth worried her lower lip. "No. He brought me all the way out here to Waterloo on the strength of that paper, then couldn't get it. I don't understand . . . "

"Neither do I, sister, but — " Sam Cragg broke off and whirled as the telephone suddenly rang. He leaped for the instrument and jerked it off the hook. "Sam Cragg talking!"

"Yeah," laughed a harsh voice. "Well, listen, we want that hunk of paper and we want it quick."

"You can have the damn thing if you'll let Johnny Fletcher go."

"We'll let him go after we get the paper."

"Nix, you let him go first. How do I know . . . ?" Sam stiffened. "How do I know that he's still all right?"

"Well, just hang on a minute. Hey . . . !"

Then Johnny Fletcher's calm voice came on the phone. "Hello, Sammy. I'm no lousy hero, bring the paper where they tell you."

"It's at — " Johnny began and was cut off. The harsh voice came on again.

"All right, we've had enough clowning. It's three twenty-eight. You be standing right on the curve where Highway 28 turns to go around Janesville — going west — at exactly four o'clock. Have that hunk of paper or you ain't goin' to see your wise guy pal again. Catch on?"

"Yeah, sure," cried Sam, "but look, I ain't got a car and I haven't got a dime. How'm I going to get there — ?"

"That's your worry. I'll give you until four-fifteen. Walk if you have to."

Sam hung up the receiver and turned to Jill Thayer. "Where the heck's Janesville?"

286

"Fifteen miles from here."

Sam groaned. "I've got to be there in forty-five minutes and I haven't got a car or a dime to my name to hire one."

"I've got the money and the car," Jill Thayer said, promptly.

"Huh? You mean you'll help . . . ?"

"Of course! I've been using my uncle's car. It's across the street in the parking lot. I can have you in Janesville in less than a half hour. That's plenty of time . . . mmm, I want you to talk to my cousin, Tommy Johnson."

"How do you mean — talk?"

"He hasn't been honest with me."

A slow grin came to Sam's harassed face. "You mean I should kinda *make* him talk?"

"He's in Room 415."

Sam Cragg smacked his big hands together and strode to the door. Jill Thayer followed him, frowning. When she got to the hall, Sam was pounding on the door of Room 415.

"All right, me boy, open up!" he boomed. "I know you're in there and it won't do you no good to keep quiet."

The door was jerked open by the angry-faced Tommy Johnson. "Look here, you big walrus," he began and then Sam Cragg shoved him into the room. Inside he continued to shove until he had slammed Tommy Johnson against a wall.

"I hear you been telling fibs, Tommy," he said. "And somebody else told me you useta have sticky fingers. Now, that ain't nice at all; first thing you know you're going to tell real big lies and get into serious trouble. So . . . " Sam slapped Tommy's face with the back of his hand.

Behind Sam, Jill Thayer exclaimed sharply, "Don't!"

Tommy Johnson cried out hoarsely and swung at Sam with his fist, Sam rolled with the blow and took it on his shoulder. He stepped back and, catching hold of Tommy by the coat front, shook him violently back and forth.

"I ain't got time to fool around with you, Tommy," he snapped. "You'll come clean or by gosh I'll shake your ears loose from your head . . . "

"You go to — !"

Whack!

Sam slapped Tommy Johnson with his free hand, let Tommy take another futile punch at him, then slapped him again. Tommy sagged in his grip and began whimpering.

"Let me go, I didn't do anything to you . . . "

"No? Maybe because of you my pal Johnny Fletcher's getting the business right now. Talk and talk damn quick."

"Tommy," said Jill Thayer, "How did you first find out about the Shellrock High School paper?"

"So you're siding with him," Tommy moaned, bitterly. "You'd doublecross your own cousin."

"Nix on that, little man," said Sam cheerfully. "Miss Jill couldn't stop me if she tried. Not when Johnny Fletcher's life is at stake. Answer the question or — "

He drew back his hand, but Tommy screamed. "I'll tell. I was working for Ned Lester and came across a stack of old school papers in his attic. They didn't mean anything to me at that time, but when I went to New York and heard that Blockhead was making all that money I remembered seeing the same cartoon in the school paper. At least I thought it was the same cartoon, but I wasn't sure."

"It was the same, Tommy," said Jill. "Go on."

"That's all. You know the rest, Jill. I told you and — "

"And what about Egbert Craddock?"

"I never knew him!"

"Whoa!" cried Sam. "He came to your room the day he was knocked off."

Tommy Johnson's knees suddenly collapsed under him so suddenly that he tore free of Sam Cragg's grip and fell to the floor. Sam shot a quick glance at Jill Thayer and saw her staring down at her cousin, an expression of horror on her face.

"Oh-oh!" said Sam. He reached down and with a jerk lifted Tommy Johnson to his feet. "Go on, pal. Spill the rest."

"There isn't any more," Tommy Johnson moaned.

Jill Thayer said in a dead voice, "You told Craddock about the paper."

"No — no, I didn't. Honest, I didn't — "

Whack!

"Don't lie to the lady," Sam Cragg snarled.

"Let him go, Sam," Jill said listlessly. "Let him go. We've got to start anyway, or we'll be late . . . "

Sam Cragg let Tommy Johnson fall to the floor. "Jeez, I almost forgot for a minute. Come on . . . "

He and Jill hurried from the hotel to the parking lot and across the street. Jill gave her check to the attendant and a

Buick coupe was rolled out.

"Hang on," said Jill, after she climbed behind the wheel and Sam was beside her.

She shot the coupe out of the lot, narrowly missing a bus. She made a quick turn, zoomed the car two blocks to the main highway out of town and then gave it the gas.

They rolled down Rainbow Drive to Cedar Falls at better than sixty miles an hour and once through the little city hit it up to seventy-five.

After five or six minutes, Jill took her foot off the accelerator. "There's your corner up there. I'll let you off."

"Where are you going?"

"I'll cruise past a couple of miles, then turn and come back. I won't stop until you signal me. I'll go fairly fast, so no one will suspect me. Okay?"

Sam nodded. "Yeah — and thanks — Jill!"

"Good luck, Sam!"

She braked the car to a stop and let Sam out of the car at the turn in the road. Sam watched the car shoot off, then looked around. To the north and west he could see the houses of a small village, but where he stood there wasn't a single house within a quarter of a mile.

19

JOHNNY FLETCHER'S ride, after being kidnaped at the point of a gun, was a short, but thrilling one. Sitting in the tonneau of the limousine with the revolver inches from his body, he clung to the seat rest as the car roared over the rough graveled road at better than sixty miles an hour.

It made several sharp turns, during which the tires screeched and the car plowed up clouds of dust. Then suddenly, after less than five minutes of riding, the car was braked to a stop.

"Out," the gunman ordered Johnny and prodded him with the revolver.

The thugs piled out after Johnny and rushed him toward a weatherbeaten roadhouse that stood a short distance from the highway. Johnny had a quick glimpse of the wooden sign, *The Green Spot*.

They entered the place by a rear door and were met by a burly man in a grimy apron.

"Any customers, Jake?" the man with gun asked.

"Naw, too early, but keep him quiet just the same. Anyone follow you?"

"No, we fixed that. Henry, change the license plates."

"Okay, Mac." The man who had driven the car darted outside. The man called Mac prodded Johnny Fletcher. "Upstairs, punk!"

Johnny climbed a creaky flight of stairs to a narrow hall, which led to a fairly large room at the front of the roadhouse. It contained a cheap chiffonier, a roll-top desk, a couple of chairs and a bed on which was spread a moth-eaten army blanket.

"How long you figure on keeping him here, Mac?" asked Jake, the roadhouse man.

"That depends; frisk him."

Jake came around behind Johnny Fletcher and while Mac held a gun on Johnny went thoroughly through the latter's pockets. He yelped joyfully when he found the roll of bills Johnny had obtained at the Red Windmill.

"Jeez, Santa Claus!"

"Swell," said Mac, "That'll take care of the overhead. But find the paper."

"Oh, that," said Johnny. "I haven't got it."

"The hell you haven't!"

"Uh-huh, but go ahead, look."

Jake finished his search. "If he's hiding more'n a two cent stamp, Mac, I'll eat it."

Mac advanced upon Johnny and put his revolver into Johnny's stomach. "I'll give you up to three to tell me where it is . . . One . . . "

"Whoa," cried Johnny. "I don't need three. My big pal's got it."

Mac swore without heat. "It *would* be tough. He's probably heading back for Waterloo, now. No . . . he'll run back to the Red Windmill . . . Mmm . . . "

He nodded to Jake. "Call the Red

Windmill at Shellrock. Ask for Sam Cragg."

"They'll trace the call, Mac!"

"We won't be on long enough. Anyway, they won't trace it. I'll make that clear."

Jake shook his head but went to the roll-top desk and, sliding up the top, picked up a telephone. He called a number, then said, "Red Windmill? Say, is there a man there named Sam Cragg? Yeah . . . Fine!"

Mac crossed the room swiftly and handed his gun to Jake. Then he took the telephone and spoke to Sam Cragg. He ordered Johnny to the telephone, but stood over him while he spoke.

When he slammed down the receiver he snarled at Johnny. "Makes it damn complicated. Why couldn't you just have the thing with you?"

"Made it too easy for you. Pretty easy as it is."

"Wise guy, huh?"

"Not with that gun in your mitt. Naturally, I'm sore. I won that twelve hundred and fifty-eight dollars fair and square and I hadn't even got to warm it up. Look, you can't be getting much more for this other job. Why don't we make a deal? I'll let you keep half the money and not say a word."

"I can keep it all," said Mac, "and fix you so you won't say a word. You should have stayed in New York. I hear this wasn't any of your business anyway."

"No more so than yours, Mac. You're in it for some dough, aren't you? Well, that's why I got into it."

"No one was paying you."

"That's what *you* think. I had a darned good paying customer. Mm, what're you getting for that paper?"

"Enough."

"If it's less than two grand you'd better let *me* sell it. I'll get five."

"Five thousand?"

Johnny saw Henry scowling at Mac. "Yep," he said, cheerfully, "I might even kick it up to ten thou. There's a lot of dough tied up in it."

"You're crazy, it's only a high school paper."

"So it is, but do you know what's in it?"

"What could be in it that's worth that much money?"

"Do you ever watch television — Blockhead, the strong man . . . ?"

"Blockhead!" exclaimed Henry, coming into the room.

"Yeah, sure, every night at six-thirty. Good program."

"Do *you* ever watch it?" Johnny asked Mac.

"I've seen it. What's it got to do with this?"

"Plenty. You know that Blockhead is on the air. Do you know that there's a comic magazine drawn around Blockhead and a strip that appears in a lot of newspapers . . . ?"

"So what?"

"So Blockhead made a million bucks for the guy who owns the copyright. That little Shellrock school paper can take the million away from the fellow."

"I don't get it!"

"I'll draw you a picture. Blockhead popped up a year or two ago. A guy by the name of Matt Boyce claims to own Blockhead. But — some high school kid over here in Shellrock originated Blockhead twelve years ago. The first strip was printed in the school paper."

"Who drew it?"

"Who put you up to his job?"

Mac scowled. "Nobody you know."

"A fat guy in Waterloo. Name of Langford."

"Never heard of him. What makes you think he sicked me onto you?"

"Because he sold the paper too cheap."

"How much did he charge you?"

"Only two fifty. I'd have given him five hundred just as easy. Maybe more."

"Why, the fat slob!" cried Henry. "He's holding out on us."

"Shut your trap, Henry," snapped Mac. "This wise guy may be stringing us."

"Could be," grinned Johnny.

"Could be," sneered Mac and stepping forward suddenly smashed Johnny in the face with his fist. Johnny reeled back, caught his balance and started to charge, but Mac stuck out his revolver.

"Put it down," said Johnny, angrily, "Put it down and I'll beat your brains out."

"Okay," said Mac, "I'll put it down." He stuck the gun into his hip pocket, then as Johnny started forward, "Henry!"

Johnny lashed out with his left fist, but Mac stepped nimbly aside. Johnny whirled and took a high blow on his forehead. It staggered him back — into the big fist of Henry, which caught him on the right kidney.

He gasped in pain, turned to strike at Henry and took a devastating blow on his jaw from Mac. He fell to his knees and started to shake his head to clear away the buzzing. In that position Mac's foot caught him on the left temple.

Red pain exploded in his head. It

was so fierce that he cried out and the pain dissolved into blackness. Then it came back and he struggled to his knees. He raised his head and looked into the porcine face of Langford, the bookdealer.

"The boys play rough," the bookdealer wheezed. "You shouldn't ought to make them mad."

"He says he paid you two-fifty," Mac accused.

"Did he say that? Tsk. Tsk. And how much did you find on him?"

"Huh?"

"He broke the bank at the Red Windmill."

"Oh, your stooge Clem Meeker told you, huh?"

"Of course. Twelve hundred and fifty-eight dollars. Let me have it."

"Hey," cried Henry.

"That wasn't part of the deal," Mac said evenly. "Nothing was said about what we picked up on the side."

"No, because I didn't know he'd have money like that. I, uh, was under the impression he was rather flat. But twelve hundred. Very well, you're entitled to a share. Three into twelve fifty-eight."

"Three?"

"Henry, you and uh, me."

"What about Jake?"

"Mmm, he's taking no risks. We're merely using his place for convenience. Well, we'll give him the fifty-eight. Split the twelve hundred three ways."

"And the money you're going to pay us for the job?"

Langford sighed. "You boys have been doing all right, working for me, haven't you? Don't let success go to your heads. I promised you five hundred between you. You're getting eight. Isn't that enough?"

"No," said Mac.

"Damn right, no," cried Henry.

"You're driving a hard bargain, boys."

"So's he," Johnny Fletcher cut in. "He's getting ten thousand from New York."

The eyes of both Mac and Henry came to Johnny. The fat man shook his head. "Uh, Mac, what were you doing when I came in?"

"Slapping him silly."

"Maybe you slapped him too hard — or not hard enough."

"Maybe," said Mac. "But just for fun, how much are you getting from New York?"

"One thousand dollars and there'll be the expense of taking it to New York."

Johnny snickered. "Believe that and you're dopes!"

Langford turned to Johnny. "Mr. Fletcher, I don't believe I like you."

"I don't like you either."

"I shall remember that, later. Mac, isn't it time to make that telephone call?"

"Just about. All right, sucker. You're going to talk to your sidekick again."

"I don't feel like talking to him . . . Wait a minute, okay."

"Thanks, pal. You're getting smart."

Mac went to the phone and made the call to the hotel in Waterloo.

He got Sam and again made Johnny say his piece. When he finally hung up on Sam he looked inquiringly at Langford. "That's not very far from here."

"No, it isn't," said Langford. "This chap is a little more difficult than I'd expected. And Clem Meeker tells me that the Cragg fellow practically broke up the Red Windmill."

"Sammy did?" Johnny cried. "Good for him."

"Maybe not. Mmm, McClusky, I think you'd better bring him here. But be careful. Meeker says he's a very powerful man."

"You're telling me?" Henry put in. "I'm going to use a blackjack on his noggin and ask questions afterward."

"I wouldn't if I were you," Johnny warned.

"But you ain't."

20

SEVERAL cars passed Sam Cragg as he stood on the road shoulder of Highway 218. One car even slowed down and a man called out, asking if he wanted a lift.

It was five minutes after four when Jill Thayer shot past headed in the direction of Waterloo. She made no sign that she even saw him.

Another car came along in a few minutes, a battered red coupé that had once been bright red, but was now faded and mud-spattered. It started to swing out as if to pass Sam, then suddenly braked to a halt.

Mac leaped out of the car, his revolver held in front of him. "Got the paper?" he cried.

"Yeah sure, where's Johnny?"

"He'll be turned loose in ten minutes.

Let's have the paper. And damn quick!"

Sam Cragg reached for his breast pocket. "Here it is," he said, holding out the copy of the Shellrock *Hi-Way*. "Take it and hurry . . . " He reeled back as Mac suddenly crashed the barrel of the revolver on his head.

He sat down heavily on the road shoulder. Mac exclaimed in chagrin and lunged forward. Sam saw him coming and rolled to one side. The second blow of the revolver caught him on the shoulder, upsetting him. But even as he fell he snaked out one hand and caught Mac's ankle. He jerked on it and Mac hit the pavement. He cried out in terror.

"I told you so!" screamed Henry, diving from behind the wheel. There was a blackjack in his hand. He swung it viciously at Sam's head.

The weapon landed squarely on Sam's head with such force that the leather burst and lead shot showered over him. He fell forward, groaning, and then Mac got in one more blow with the revolver. Sam slumped into unconsciousness, but even then Mac hit him again.

When he got up he was trembling. "Jeez, the guy's a reg'lar elephant."

"D'you see that billy bust on his head?" Henry asked in awe.

"There's a car coming back a couple of miles," exclaimed Mac. "Hurry, we've got to get him into the bus."

The two men tugged and hauled on Sam and lifted him into the coupé, sitting him up between them. A passing car would not see anything amiss in three men in a coupé, one of them apparently sleeping.

They got away before the approaching car was within a half mile, then they lost the car in a burst of speed that reached seventy-five miles an hour by the time they took the second Janesville turn and hit the straightaway, leading to Waverly, six miles away.

They drove clear through Waverly and a mile or so beyond, where the red coupé was jerked off the pavement and rolled in behind the Green Spot Tavern.

They parked the car close by the rear door and Jake opened it almost immediately. "Quiet," he said. "A couple of truck drivers are having some coffee out in front."

"Why didn't you tell them you were closed?" Mac snapped.

"Couldn't they're oldtimers and they know me. They won't stay long. Lug him upstairs."

Mac and Henry slid Sam out of the coupé, dropping him once upon the ground. Sam began kicking feebly as they ascended the stairs, and Henry cried out in fright. But Sam was still unconscious when they took him nto the room where Langford sat overflowing a large rocking chair with a gun trained on Johnny Fletcher, across the room.

They dumped Sam on the floor and Johnny, disregarding Langford's gun, shot up and leaped to Sam's side. He exclaimed in dismay when he saw the wounds on Sam.

"You . . . !" he said bitterly to Mac and Henry.

Mac kicked viciously at Johnny. "Outta the way, I ain't takin' no chances with this gorilla."

He tossed a coil of washline to the floor and began lashing Sam Cragg's ankles. Finished, he jerked Sam's wrists together behind his back, tying them securely, then ran a length of rope from the wrists to the ankles, pulling them together before finally tying a knot.

"Now, let him wake up!"

Almost as if he heard, Sam opened his eyes. He blinked, saw Johnny Fletcher's anxious face and yelped, "Cripes, how'd you get back so soon . . . I mean, holy cow!" He struggled for a moment, then let out a yell. "Hey, what's the idea?"

Mac thrust a gun down into Sam's face. "One more yip out of you and I'll slip you a slug."

Henry came within the range of

Sam's eyes. "Breakin' my blackjack with your head!"

Langford cleared his throat noisily. "Quiet, please." He tapped the copy of the Shellrock *Hi-Way*. "Do you know a man named Enoch Holtzman, Fletcher?"

"No, am I supposed to?"

"I thought you looked at this cartoon strip?"

"I didn't have to. I knew what it would be — a cartoon of Blockhead, the Strong Man."

"Yes, but you don't know who Holtzman is?"

"I do," said Sam Cragg. "The guy who drew the funny picture. And you know what, Johnny, Jill Thayer knows who Holtzman is. She didn't let on, but she knows."

Langford frowned so that his eyes were virtually lost in rolls of flesh. "Have you shown this to the Thayer girl?"

"Yeah, she said — "

"She went back to New York on

the afternoon train," Johnny cut in quickly.

Langford grunted. "That's a lie. I know more about Miss Jill Thayer than either of you. Her cousin, Tommy — "

" . . . Is a worm!"

"A louse," said Langford. "But he's been useful to me in a business way. He sent me a couple of good customers."

"Me and Egbert Craddock, I suppose."

"And another one, indirectly. The squirt didn't know that he was playing with dynamite and tried a little blackmail. Lucky he hasn't got his fingers burned yet."

"I'll chop them off when I see him again," Johnny said, savagely.

"*When* you see him again," Mac put in ironically.

"Huh?"

"You heard me. Have you thought it over, Langford? We're getting peanuts and your New York customer has a million bucks."

"I've been thinking about it,

312

McCluskey, and I see your point. I not only see it, but I anticipated it. I gave him a jingle on the long distance telephone before I came out here. He's sweating right now. I said I'd call him again tonight. He intimated that he was all right on that end, but didn't like this end. He named Mr. Fletcher."

"How much?"

"He offered another thousand. I'm holding out for more."

"He'll kick through with ten."

"Hey," said Johnny. "Are you fellows discussing me?"

"Be quiet, Fletcher," said Langford, "or we'll have to gag you. I don't know, McCluskey, if he'll go up to ten. I don't think he's got it."

He'll jolly well have to get it. This job's worth it. We're taking a lot of risk."

"Wait a minute, fellows," cut in Henry. "I'm as game as the next one, but murder's out of my line."

"Hey!" cried Sam Cragg. "What're you talking about — murder?"

"Shut your trap," snarled Mac.

"I won't," howled Sam Cragg. "I don't like knocking around any too much, but when you start talking about murder and me the guy who's to get it — "

"I said shut up!" McCluskey whipped up his revolver and advanced on Sam Cragg.

The latter rolled over quickly and banged his heels on the floor. "Cut it out, help, police . . . !"

"Don't shot!" bleated Langford. "Those people downstairs . . . !"

"I'll knock his brains out," fumed McCluskey. "Henry, grab him."

Henry seemed dubious but stepped forward to hold Sam Cragg while McCluskey clubbed him with the revolver. Johnny Fletcher suddenly lunged forward from the bunk on which he had been sitting and hit Henry's legs with his head and shoulders. Henry plunged forward, falling over Sam Cragg.

Then Johnny Fletcher saw the thing

for which he had been half hoping: a tremendous exhibition of strength on Sam Cragg's part. Only Johnny knew the power in the big fellow's muscles.

Sam Cragg strained with his legs and arms all at the same time. The rope that bound his wrists down to this ankles snapped with a pop. Then Sam Cragg twisted his fists violently back and forth and the rope gave. It was stained with blood but Sam didn't seem to mind. He uttered a roar and shot both hands for McCluskey's ankles.

He got hold of only one and McCluskey squealed in fright. He lashed down at Sam's head with the gun, but the blow didn't land, for Sam jerked him off balance.

Johnny, about to tackle Henry, caught sight of Jake, the roadhouse owner, plunging into the room with a length of wood that looked like a small tree trunk. He yelled and threw himself at Jake. He got under the swing of the club, but Jake caught him around the waist and threw him to the floor.

In the meantime, Sam had slapped the gun out of McCluskey's hand and struggled to his knees. His ankles were still bound together, but he didn't seem to have the time to break the rope that held them together. Henry was belaboring the back of his head with both fists and McCluskey was using everything he had to fight Sam. And in front of them, obese Langford, who had previously given orders not to shoot, was following the fight on the floor, looking for a opening to send a shot at Sam with his revolver without hitting either Mac or Henry.

Johnny was having his hands full with Jake, was fighting a losing battle in fact. Sam was struggling with both Henry and Mac and trying to keep one of them before him as a shield against Langford.

The big bookdealer lumbered forward, began weaving from side to side. Sam caught sight of him and, with a sudden desperate show of strength, picked up

McCluskey bodily and hurled him at Langford. The fat man was bowled over backward and got tangled up with McClusky.

Sam half wheeled, struck Henry a savage blow in the face that spun him away like a tenpin and reaching down to his ankles caught hold of the rope and ripped it like thread. Then he bounded to his feet and leaped forward, where McCluskey and Langford were getting themselves straightened out. He swooped up McClusky with one hand, struck him with his other fist and tossed him aside.

Then he reached for the three-hundred-pound Langford. He got his hands on the man's coat but it ripped to shreds as he attempted to pull the fat man up.

Langford bleated in terror. "Don't -- hurt me. I — I can't stand pain."

"Well, whaddya know?" Sam snapped. He stooped and slapped the gun out of Langford's hand. "Get up or I'll kick you in the face."

It was a quite a struggle for Langford to get up, but he made it.

At that moment Johnny Fletcher yelled, "Sam — help!"

Sam shot a quick look over his shoulder, saw Johnny flat on his back with Jake kneeling on him reaching for his club. Sam grunted and smashed the fat Langford in the stomach with his fist. He gave the blow everything he had and his fist went into the flabby mass at least a foot.

Without waiting for Langford to fall Sam whirled and charged down upon Jake. The roadhouse man cried out hoarsely and tried to scramble off Johnny, but Johnny clung to him until Sam Cragg tore him out of his grasp and threw him halfway across the room.

Then he let out a tremendous sigh and slapped his hands together. "I haven't had a workout like that in a long time!"

Johnny got to his feet and looked around the room. He whistled in awe. "Jeez!"

Across the room Langford was sitting on the floor, his hands to his stomach, his mouth open. He was purple in the face and didn't seem to have yet caught his breath from the tremendous blow Sam had struck him.

McCluskey was lying on the floor, his mouth open and drooling saliva. He was unconscious. Nearby, Henry was trying to crawl on his hands and knees. Blood was streaming from his nose and he was moaning.

Jake was flat on his face, unconscious.

Johnny walked unsteadily across to Langford and stooping, pulled open the fat man's coat. At that moment Langford let go his breath and it was like a small cyclone. But Johnny whipped the folded high school paper from Langford's breast pocket and then turned to McCluskey.

He searched the thug's pockets and brought forth a huge roll of bills and one smaller. He counted the smaller roll. "Two ten, fine. I'll call it interest on the money he borrowed from me.

Okay, Sam, let's scram!"

"You don't want any of these monkeys?"

"No, they've had enough."

"But you don't know who the guy in New York is?"

"I knew that before we left the big town. But I didn't have the proof. That's why I came here — to get the proof. Come on, we're going home."

They took the stairs quickly to the first floor and found the shoddy restaurant deserted of customers. They pulled open the door and stepped outside just as Jill Thayer's coupé drove off the road onto the gravel.

She called to them. "Sam Cragg — Johnny Fletcher! Are you all right?"

"I feel fine," Sam Cragg exulted.

"Me, too," said Johnny. "Uh, how come you're here at this psychological moment?"

"I've been driving back and forth. I followed the car that brought Sam here and I'd made up my mind if he didn't show in another minute or two

I was going to telephone for the state police."

Johnny grinned crookedly. "From where were you going to telephone? Inside here?"

She flushed. "I — I have a gun." Her eyes darted to a purse that lay on the seat beside her.

Johnny picked it up and hefted it. The gun was pretty small. "So you were going to rescue us, single-handed? Too bad we couldn't wait. But I think just to be on the safe side we'd better get out of here as fast as we can. They've got some guns themselves."

"Jump in!"

Thirty seconds later the coupé was zooming in the direction of Waterloo.

21

THE plane from Chicago descended upon La Guardia Airport a few minutes after eight in the morning and at a quarter to nine Jill Thayer, Johnny Fletcher and Sam Cragg got out of a taxicab in front of the 45th Street Hotel.

It was too early for Peabody to be on duty, but Eddie Miller was in the lobby. He smirked when he saw the trio enter.

"Been traveling, folks?" he asked.

"We been traveling," Johnny replied. "We'll let you know when and if we want ice water."

"Swell, only I was going to tell you that the cops were around here all day yesterday. They searched your rooms and — well, you'll be hearing from them."

"*Rooms*, you say, Eddie?"

"Rooms, uh-huh. I heard them say somethin' about findin' bloodstains in Miss Thayer's trunk, but that couldn't be, could it?"

"That's ridiculous!" exclaimed Jill Thayer.

"Eddie," said Johnny grimly, "remind me come Christmas to give you a nice fat check. A rubber check . . . Going up!"

In the elevator Jill started to speak but Johnny winked at her. They all got off at the seventh floor and Jill unlocked her room.

"Oh!" she cried, when she saw the disorder.

"You'd think the clumsy mutts would put things back," Johnny said in disgust.

"Well, they couldn't muss our room very much," said Sam, "on account of we haven't got anything to muss up."

Jill turned to Johnny, a worried look on her face. "What are you going to do?"

"I don't know yet. I want to size up

the situation. Things may have been happening while we were away. I'm going to get cleaned up, then grab some breakfast. I suppose you'll be here a while?"

"Of course. I've got to make some phone calls. I ran out on my work, you know. There was a deadline, too."

"I'll telephone you."

Johnny and Sam climbed the stairs to the eighth floor and Johnny put the key into the door of Room 821. It turned but the door didn't open. He pushed on it and rattled the doorknob then tried the key again.

This time the key turned, but it wasn't necessary for Johnny to push the door. It was pulled open from the inside.

Jefferson Todd looked down on Johnny from his height.

"So you're back!"

"Hey!" cried Sam Cragg. "What the devil you doin' in our room?"

"*Your* room? This is mine. I rented it last night."

"You're crazy, Jefferson," Johnny snapped. "We're paid in advance on this room."

"I wouldn't know about that, I asked for a room and this is the one they gave me. I'm afraid you'll have to take it up with the management."

Sam Cragg reached out with a big hand and brushed Todd to one side. He strode into the room and looked for their trunk. It was gone.

"Why, the dirty . . . ! Wait'll I see Peabody."

"I guess he thought you'd run out. After all, with the police searching for you all over and — "

"That's a lie, Jefferson. The cops didn't want us. Lieutenant Madigan gave us a clear bill."

"Did he? Maybe he changed his mind. Seems to me I heard something about his finding bloodstains — bloodstains that had been washed — in Miss Thayer's trunk. I believe he's going to hold you two as material witnesses. At least."

"At least, nothing, I can wash up Madigan's case any time I want."

"Eh?" Jefferson Todd's lean body leaned forward and his big Adam's apple moved up and down. "Where were you, anyway?"

"Iowa, where the tall corn grows."

"Iowa . . . say, that rare book-dealer — "

"I think he went out of business yesterday. You'd have liked him, Jefferson. He was as fat as you were skinny. You coulda gone in business with him."

"Haw haw!" roared Sam Cragg.

Jefferson Todd flushed angrily. "Have your little joke, boys. But I think I've solved the case myself."

"Don't tell me now," said Johnny, snapping his fingers. "The murderer was Blockhead, the Strong Man."

"Accessory only. Craddock was a blackmailer. He was blackmailing Boyce and Dan Murphy. You remember they were in business together once. Craddock took the rap and went to prison. When he came out Boyce had gotten rid of Murphy and was riding high. Craddock cut himself in and Boyce didn't like it. So — Pfft!"

"And then Boyce committed suicide?"

Jefferson Todd sniffed. "I said Murphy, Boyce and Craddock were all partners originally in that blackmail sheet. Murphy was out of it, but couldn't squawk about Boyce without involving himself. For blackmail. But murder was something else. When Boyce killed Craddock, Murphy got scared and beat Boyce to it."

"Could be," said Johnny Fletcher. "Could be. Boyce hired us to get divorce evidence against his wife, he knew she was carrying on with Murphy. Mmm, and Lulu inherits Boyce's dough. A million bucks. What does Madigan think of your theory?"

"I haven't told him. He can't see anything but the blood in the Thayer girl's trunk. That's simple enough. Ken Ballinger lives here at the hotel and Craddock came here often enough.

Naturally, Boyce wasn't going to bump him at his office. he followed him here . . . "

" . . . And lured him into Jill's room!"

Jefferson Todd's eyes glittered. "After all, all murder evidence is circumstantial. Murderers don't perform to audiences. They — "

Someone fell against the half-opened door and Ken Ballinger staggered into the room.

"Here y'are," he exclaimed drunkenly. "So you ran off with my girl, huh? Cuttin' in on me, huh? Nobody c'n do that t' me and getaway with it. Nobody — "

He swung at Johnny Fletcher, but Johnny was a good six feet away, beyond Jefferson Todd, so it was Todd who took Ken's swing. The blow struck him glancingly on the jaw.

"Be damned!" cried Sam Cragg. "I never saw a guy who gets drunk before breakfast."

"You drunken hoodlum," Jefferson

Todd said angrily. "I've a good notion to — "

"Go ahead, see what it'll get you. And you, Blockhead, I'll chop you down to my size. I made you, see, and I can cut you down."

"What a man!" Sam breathed, admiringly.

Ken Ballinger lumbered up to Sam Cragg, took deliberate aim and fired a punch at Sam's head. Sam half turned and rolled with the blow. He took it on the shoulder, yawned and waited for Ken to swing at him again. Ken did and the fist landed on Sam's jaw.

Johnny, watching in amusement, saw Sam's eyes pop wide. Then Sam struck out with his open fist and bowled Ken Ballinger back into Jefferson Todd. Todd crashed against the wall and howled.

"Cut it out, you hoodlums. Get out of my room."

Johnny winked at Sam and the latter, aroused, advanced on Jefferson Todd and shoved him out of the room. "This is our room, Todd. Stay out of it. And that goes for Peabody, too. Tell him I said so."

"I'm going to murder you, Blockhead," Ken Ballinger bawled, drunkenly. "You can't knock me around, I'm getting sick and tired of being pushed around and I ain't gonna stand for it, see?"

"I wouldn't either, if I was you, Kennie boy," said Sam and shoved Ballinger out of the room after Jefferson Todd. He bolted the door on the inside. "Imagine a guy gettin' drunk before breakfast."

"Maybe he doesn't know it's breakfast time," Johnny said. "He might still be going from last night. Do you know, we've never yet seen Ken Ballinger when he wasn't drunk."

"That's right, we haven't. And speaking of breakfast, I could do with some. Those little snacks they served on the airplane hardly touched bottom."

"Yeah, but if we leave this room we

330

may get dispossessed again."

"Like to see Peabody try it. I'm getting sore, Johnny. People are picking on me."

"Just like Ken Ballinger. He says people are picking on him."

"That's his own fault. But it ain't mine. You ready to eat?"

"Yes, let's go."

They left Room 821 and rode down in the elevator. They encountered Peabody just about to step in. Jefferson Todd was ducking out of the hotel.

"Fletcher," groaned Peabody, "I'd hoped you were gone for good."

"So you could go south with the advance room rent? Sorry, old man. I'll thank you to get rid of that Todd person's luggage and return ours to our room . . . after you fumigate the room."

"I should never have got into the hotel business," wailed the hotel manager. "I suppose I can expect murder and all sorts of things now that you're back."

"No more murders, Peabody. A little mayhem maybe, but . . . " Johnny left the sentence unfinished and headed for the door.

They went to a cafeteria across the street and each had a substantial breakfast. When they came out it was twenty minutes to ten.

"Now, let's go see the Blockhead gang," Johnny said. "Taxi!"

A few minutes later they climbed out before the big building that contained the offices of the Boyce Publishing Company. They rode up in the elevator and entered the luxurious reception room.

Johnny smiled pleasantly at the receptionist. "Remember me? Like to see the boss."

"Mrs. Boyce?"

"That's right."

"About what did you want to see her?"

"Uh, about Dan Murphy."

"Perhaps it's Mr. Murphy you want to see, then."

"Oh, is he here . . . already? All right, announce me to him."

"Your name?"

"Same as it was the other day, Fletcher."

22

THE receptionist closed the little glass window. She kept it closed after speaking into the telephone, but in a moment or two the door was opened by Dan Murphy.

"What do you want, Fletcher?" he asked truculently.

"Congratulations."

"On what?"

"On moving in. You didn't waste any time."

"Get the hell outta here. And stay away."

"Oh, a tough guy," said Sam Cragg.

Murphy took a step back and caught hold of the doorknob. "You're not going to pick a fight with me."

"Oh, we weren't thinking of that at all," said Johnny. "I just dropped in to tell you that you're going to lose Blockhead."

With the door halfway open Murphy turned. "What's that?"

"Why, you're going to be sued on Blockhead. Plagiarism."

"What're you talking about?"

Johnny smiled pleasantly. "Shall we go in?"

Murphy hesitated only a moment. "Come on."

He led the way down the long hall to the office that had been Matt Boyce's and entered without knocking. Lulu Boyce, looking more gorgeous than ever, sat in her late husband's swivel chair.

"Ah, Mr. Fletcher!" she exclaimed. "And Blockhead!"

"How're you, Mrs. Boyce?" said Johnny. "Gee, if all business offices were like this I'd go into business myself."

"Go ahead, Mr. Fletcher," Lulu Boyce invited. "I love your line. Go right ahead while I make a telephone call. The police, you know I understand they're looking for you."

"Wait a minute, Lu," Dan Murphy interrupted. "He was squawking about somebody slapping a suit on you. For plagiarism."

"Plagiarism? What's that?"

Johnny chuckled. "Oh, that's bad. It seems that Boyce Publications swiped the Blockhead idea and the real owner is going to sue you. If he wins he'll get all the dough that Blockhead has ever earned."

"Pooh!"

Johnny took the copy of the Shellrock *Hi-Way* from his pocket and opening it to the Blockhead cartoon moved up to Lulu Boyce's desk. He leaned over and held the paper so Lulu could see the cartoon. He watched her face and saw the color fade from her cheeks.

"Where'd you get that?" she asked after a moment.

"It's a high school paper. The date is 1952 — twelve years ago; about ten years before Blockhead blossomed out here."

"Let me see that paper," Murphy cried.

Johnny turned and showed it, but would not let Murphy get within reaching distance. Murphy began to swear. "*I* started Blockhead. Matt Boyce stole it from me."

"And where'd *you* steal it?"

"I didn't steal it. Ken Ballinger created the idea. He was working for me on a salary and naturally the idea became the property of the firm."

"But the name on this strip is Enoch Holtzman."

"Who the hell is Enoch Holtzman?"

"He was a boy who went to the Shellrock High School . . . twelve years ago."

"Twelve years ago, yeah, but where is he now? Is he the monkey that's going to sue?"

"Yep. After looking at this do you think he's got a good case?"

"That's a phony paper. It could be forged."

"No, the entire class of 1952 of the Shellrock High School will be brought up as witnesses. And — this is copyrighted. You haven't a leg to stand on!"

"Let them sue!" cried Lulu Boyce. "I'll fight them until — "

"Wait a minute, Lu," said Murphy. "Let's talk this over. Fletcher, where'd you get that paper?"

"In Iowa. That's where I was yesterday."

"How come you went out there? Where do you come in on all this?"

"Why, two men were killed. Egbert Craddock and — "

"No!" shuddered Lulu Boyce.

"Yes, Egbert Cradock got one of these papers and was killed the same day. Then Matt — "

"Hold on, Fletcher. Your story doesn't hold water. If this Enoch Holtzman has such a good case, why'd he want to knock off Matt? Craddock, I can understand. Maybe he was going to shake down Matt. He served time for that once. But how could the guy collect by knocking off Matt?"

"Well, that puzzled me a little, but you see . . . " Johnny stopped as the phone whirred on Lulu Boyce's desk and she picked up the receiver.

"Who?" she exclaimed. "No! . . . very well!" She hung up. "Mr. Fletcher, be prepared for a surprise . . . "

Behind Johnny the door was thrown open and the voice of Lieutenant Madigan boomed, "Johnny Fletcher!"

"Hi, Maddy," Johnny said. "I see Todd didn't waste any time."

"What'd you run out of town for? You knew damn well I wanted you to stick around."

"Sure, but I couldn't solve your case for you here."

"No clowning, Fletcher. I'm sore. I got hauled on the carpet . . . "

"Too bad, but when you break this case they'll not only forgive you but make you a captain."

Madigan scowled and shot a quick

glance around the room. "What're you doing here, Fletcher?"

Johnny sighed. "Solving your case, like I said. Don't I always?"

Madigan had forgotten to close the door behind him and the sound of a violent commotion in the hall came into the big, private office. Sam Cragg, who was near the door, stuck out his head.

"Oh, oh, that man's here again!"

"Le'me go, Harry!" howled the drunken voice of Ken Ballinger. "Le'me go, or I'll knock your block off."

"That drunken bum," gritted Dan Murphy.

"Bring 'em in," said Johnny. "The two of 'em."

"Me?" Sam looked inquiringly at Johnny and, receiving a nod, darted out of the office.

There was a further scuffle outside, then Sam Cragg came back, shoving Ken Ballinger ahead of him. Harry Hale followed. He had a split lip that was bleeding badly.

340

"Ah-ha!" Ken Ballinger cried bitterly. "So they're all here, the buzzards picking the bones clean."

"Ballinger," said Murphy, furiously, "you're through here."

"I quit the day before yesterday," Ballinger retorted. "I quit before you became the boss and you know what I think of you?"

"Shut up, Ballinger," Lieutenant Madigan growled. "I'm getting kind of fed up having you stagger in everywhere and shoot off your drunken mouth."

"I don't mind," Sam Cragg chuckled. "He keeps me in exercise."

"Blockhead," Ken Ballinger snarled, "you!"

Sam advanced on Ballinger, but Johnny waved him back. "All right, folks," he announced loudly, "since you're all here, we may as well go over this story once more. As I understand it, Murphy, Ballinger was working for you when he created — no, I can't say created — when he first drew the Blockhead strip for you. Is that right?"

"Yes. That was less than three years ago."

"Correct, and you've seen this high school paper dated twelve years ago which contains the same kind of cartoon, with the exact same title, Blockhead, the Strong Man."

"Let me see that," Lieutenant Madigan yelped, snatching for the paper. Johnny let him have it.

"I'll be damned," said Madigan.

"You should be. Look, Ken, did you ever see this high school paper?"

"It's a lie," Ken Ballinger cried. "A dirty, filthy lie!"

"Could be, but that remains to be seen. Ever hear of Enoch Holtzman?"

"No," said Ken.

Johnny wheeled suddenly on Harry Hale. "Did you?"

Hale gulped. "N-no." but his face betrayed the lie.

"You don't know Enoch Holtzman? Mmm, very well then . . . *how long has Ken Ballinger been drunk?*"

"Wh-what . . . ?"

"Fletcher," said Ken Ballinger. He brought his right hand out of his pocket and it contained a .32 automatic. This was the first time Johnny had ever seen Ballinger sober. Rather it was the first time he had seen Ken when the latter had not been acting drunk.

Lieutenant Madigan exclaimed in chagrin. "Put down that gun, Ballinger."

"Make me," said Ballinger. "Go ahead, you've got a rod on you. See if you can draw it . . . before I put a slug into your head."

"Enoch Holtzman," said Fletcher, "I don't blame you for changing your name when you became an artist. I suppose that's how you got the idea for Blockhead."

"Yeah," sneered Ballinger, "Wooden man, Blockhead. Holtzman means 'wooden man.' Damn you, Fletcher, why'd you ever come to the 45th Street Hotel?"

"Why'd you ever stuff Egbert

343

Craddock into my trunk?"

"Because I had to. I couldn't leave it in Jill's."

"No, I guess not. You killed him in her room, then you got scared and ran out. After thinking it over you came back and moved the body to my room. You shouldn't ought to have done that."

"I should have killed you and stuffed *you* into the trunk, Ballinger said, bitterly. "Now I've lost the game and have to run out."

"You can't get away, Ballinger," Madigan warned. "The minute you leave this office — "

"You're coming with me, copper. Fletcher, get his gun. No . . . I don't trust you. Harry, you do it. And be damned careful."

Harry Hale was licking his lips in terror. Ballinger laughed harshly. *You* knew my real name, Harry. That's what comes of having friends. Careful, Harry . . . "

The art director approached Madigan

cautiously and patting his hips found that Madigan's gun was in a holster in his right hip pocket. He raised the policeman's coat-tail and removed the gun gingerly.

At that moment Sam Cragg took a step forward. Instantly Ballinger's gun swiveled to cover Cragg. "Move again, Blockhead. You've got it coming to you, anyway. You and that smart friend of yours."

"Give it up, Ken," Johnny Fletcher said. "You didn't have a chance from the start."

"The hell I didn't. I would have gotten every nickel Boyce had — left! Blockhead was my idea. He made a million dollars and what did I get out of him?"

"Your wages."

"Forty dollars a week when I started," Ballinger cried. "You, Murphy, you beat me down . . . "

"You should have said that Blockhead was an old idea of yours . . . "

"And you'd have made me sign a

release on it. Yah, maybe you'd have given me an extra five bucks. I made Blockhead and you skimmed the cream off it; then Matt stepped in and found a whole creamery. But I would have got it. My copyright was good for years yet. I was going away and wait a while, then Enoch Holtzman was going to pop up in Iowa and start a suit. He wouldn't have to appear at the trial. His lawyer could have handled the case. And I wouldn't come into it here because I didn't have a copyright as Ballinger. Or I could have disappeared when the suit came up. Every kid I went to school with would have been a witness. The suit was a cinch and then . . . then you, Fletcher, queered the whole thing. All right, I'm licked, I'm lighting out without a dollar to my name. But *you* aren't going to be laughing, Fletcher. You aren't going to be laughing at all . . . "

"Don't shoot, Jefferson," Johnny Fletcher cried suddenly.

Ballinger jerked as if to whirl, then

caught himself. "You can't fool me with an old one like that . . . " he began.

Then Jefferson Todd's frightened voice spoke from the doorway. "Lieutenant . . . "

Ballinger whirled and the gun in his hand exploded. Jefferson Todd cried out in terror, but not pain . . . and then Sam Cragg slapped Ken Ballinger with his open hand. He put all his weight into the blow.

The gun flew from Ballinger's hand and Ballinger himself turned a complete somersault in the air and landed on his back eight feet away.

He kicked once or twice then lay still. Lieutenant rushed over to him, stopped, felt of his heart, then took a pair of handcuffs from his pocket and snapped them on Ballinger. He rose and sighed heavily.

"He'll be all right . . . in about a hour."

"And I thought he was drunk!" exclaimed Harry Hale.

"He put on a pretty good act," said Johnny Fletcher. "The way he kept egging Sam Cragg into slapping him was a swell touch, but dammit, I'm suspicious of guys who get drunk before breakfast . . . and I smelled his breath this morning."

Lieutenant Madigan glowered. "All right, Fletcher, That's one more I owe you. But you can't tell me that you figured that all out just because the guy's breath didn't smell of whiskey."

"Well, no, Maddy, old boy. As a matter of fact, I figured out who did it a long time ago. Only I didn't have the proof until I went out to Iowa. It couldn't have been anyone but Ballinger. He was the only one who lived at the 45th Street Hotel who had any connection with Blockhead."

"Yes, but you said Egbert was killed in the Thayer girl's room."

"That's right. He didn't want to kill him in his own room, so he took him down to Jill's — he knew she'd be out all afternoon."

"That was a dirty trick to pull on his girl!"

"That's why I never liked him."

A half hour later Johnny Fletcher and Sam Cragg left the offices of the Boyce Publishing Company. They rode quietly down in the elevator and crossed Forty-second Street to get to the Grand Central, from where they would take a shuttle subway to Times Square. As they entered the big building, Sam Cragg suddenly caught Johnny's arm.

"Say, Johnny, I just thought of something. How'd Ken Ballinger get into Jill Thayer's room without a key?"

Johnny stopped and looked sharply at Sam, then he turned and headed back to the street. Sam hurried to catch up with him.

"Where you going, Johnny?

"Over to that big art supply store."

"What for?"

"Because I just thought of the answer to that question you asked — how Ken got into Jill's room."

349

"Well, how did he?"

"He's an artist ... and so is Jill. Artists are Bohemians. They're broadminded about keys and — you know. I'm going over to buy me some brushes and paper. I'm going to dabble in art."

THE END